FOLLOW
IN HER FOOTSTEPS

written by

BROOKS ELLIS, JR

Produced by:

 **FriesenPress**

Suite 300 – 852 Fort Street

Victoria, BC, Canada V8W 1H8

www.friesenpress.com

ISBN

978-1-4602-4818-8 (Hardcover)

978-1-4602-4819-5 (Paperback)

978-1-4602-4820-1 (eBook)

1. Fiction, Family Life

Distributed to the trade by The Ingram Book Company

1

Margaret Whiting gazed out across the vast ocean as it stretched out beneath dawn's rising sun. She looked back at the blue-and-white beach house standing tall on the small hill less than sixty-yards from the shoreline and thought of her love.

Margaret walked barefoot in the sand as she held her thoughts of Richard close to her heart, and as she walked, the white sand slowly inched its way in-between her toes. Her light grayish-black hair moved in the breeze, touching her well-aged skin that kept her looking very attractive over the years. As she looked down at the flowers in her left hand, and the pair of white-ivory sandals in the other, she could almost feel Richards's warmth by her side. Margaret looked down at the white sand as she made her way towards the end of the beach; it was there where the rocks and the tall trees and the memories of her past began.

Small birds flew overhead as Margaret placed the assortment of flowers in the sand near a large rock. She then removed the old ones that have been in the sand for some time, and that were now dead. Margaret always kept one dead flower and looked at the others with sadness before she threw them into the ocean and watched them float away. As she watched them drift further and further away from the shore, she thought of herself and her sister throwing stones into the ocean as children. The two of them would try to make them skip as far as they could, but Margaret was never very good at it.

Margaret stood over the freshly-laid flowers that held all the colors of the rainbow. She then stepped back to see if they looked right to her, and they looked beautiful. She knew that her sister would have felt the same.

Margaret turned back towards the beach house––it seemed small in the sunlight shining down on it. As she looked at it, she could see two young girls running down to the beach; the image was from her past, and the two young girls were herself and her sister. The image soon faded as the sun became brighter. There was a time when the two young girls running down to the beach were Margaret's two little girls, Debbie and Stacie, but Debbie and Stacie had not played in the ocean in years; they were no longer little girls.

Margaret headed back to the beach house with the dead rose held tight in her hand, and, as soon as she walked into the house, she sat down on the chair at the foot of the staircase.

A part of her didn't want to get up, but, after a minute or two, she had to. She had never sat down on that chair after coming back from her stroll on the beach, but today she had to. It had nothing to do with her age; she was in good shape for a woman in her early fifties; she looked more like a woman who was in her early forties. It was the dead flower; she found that it was heavier than the other dead flowers she had brought back to the house over the years. It wasn't physically different; it just weighed heavier on her mind today.

She stood up and walked up the stairs and down the hall to her bedroom. She crouched down in front of the door and reached under the left side of it. Her hand came away with a small key. Margaret then unlocked the bedroom door and stepped into the dark room. She went over to the closet and stood in front of the sliding mirror doors. She just looked at herself for a moment in the glass, illuminated by a little light from the hallway.

"Margaret. Margaret," she said as she looked at herself in the mirror.

She watched her lips move as she said her name (something else that she had never done before). She then slid the closet door open and took out a light brown box, and as she did this, she knocked over a glass jar that she had covered up inside an old pillowcase.

"Damn," she said, quickly standing the glass jar back up, and then pulling the pillowcase back up over it without looking at the contents. She knew what was in it, and she didn't want to see it...not today.

She opened the box and put the dead rose inside of it, along with sheets of colored paper and the other dried-up, dead flowers. The dry flowers tried to sit up when she removed the lid, but she pushed them back down as the new one made a crunching sound. She put everything back into the closet and left the bedroom, locking the door behind her. She knew that she would have to move those colored sheets of paper someday to make room for more roses, and she would one day soon.

She didn't put the key back under the door; instead, she held it in her hand as she left the beach house for the hospital where her love Richard had been admitted two days ago on a Friday night. Margaret tried to go to the hospital as many times as she could, as many times as her heart allowed her, but it was very hard for Margaret to see Richard lying in a coma, lifeless to the world around him.

Margaret's toes held remnants of sand between them as she walked into the lobby of the hospital. It felt gritty, but not uncomfortable. By the time she reached Richard's room, the sand was on the soles of her feet. She stood outside the door for a moment to gather her thoughts; she took a deep breath, and slowly opened the door. She had hoped that he would be awake, but he wasn't. It pained her deeply, and a feeling of hurt pulled at her heart as if someone had stuck their thumb into the middle of her chest; the pain and agony was so great that it almost brought her to her knees. All she wanted was for her husband to wake up and come back to her.

Richard seemed so peaceful. His head look like it was sinking into that big fluffy pillow that Stacie had brought for him, and Margaret didn't like it. Margaret couldn't remove the pillow without a nurse to assist her with Richard. Just then, a nurse came into the room. She was very young and petite. Margaret looked her up and down, and couldn't believe that this little thing helped with anything around the hospital. Margaret couldn't see how this nurse could help another nurse move Richard out of bed, or even move him onto his side. He was a well-built man in great shape for his age. He was about six-feet tall, and he weighed about two-ten.

"Hello," the nurse said.

"Hello," Margaret replied. "How has he been? Has the doctor been to see him yet since the surgery?" Margaret asked with a quick tongue.

"The doctor actually wants to talk to you about Mr. Whiting's condition," the nurse told Margaret.

"Do you think I could get a better pillow for my husband?" Margaret asked.

"His daughter brought that pillow for him. It's better for his neck, and firm enough for him," the nurse told Margaret.

"I didn't ask you who brought it. I already know who brought it. I'm asking you for a new one," Margaret's quick tongue snapped back. "Can you not see that his head is sinking right into this one?"

"Mrs. Whiting," the doctor said as he walked into the room, stopping the nurse from replying.

"Is he going to be okay? Margaret asked in a low voice, pushing the thought of that pillow out of her mind.

"I want you to know that Mr. Whiting is still in a state of unconsciousness, and even though we have reduced the swelling in his head, it may take some time before he comes out of the coma. His recovery should have been sooner, but the brain just needs more time. I'm monitoring his condition very closely," Dr. Mann assured her.

It was hard for Margaret to hold any hope in her heart. She knew that if Richard didn't come out of the coma soon, that he maybe lost within that unconscious state for a long time. Dr. Mann told her that he would be in touch with her as things progressed. He asked her if there was anything else that she would like to know, but she didn't answer him as she took a hold of Richard's hand. Dr. Mann didn't say anything else. He walked out of the room and stood in the doorway for a moment; the petite nurse walked past him on her way to get a new pillow. Margaret looked back at him as he glanced at her; her eyes showed him nothing but sadness, pain, and anger. Margaret knew she had to be strong for the family, and for Richard. She also knew that her oldest daughter would be there for her if she were to fall too far into melancholy.

Margaret sat down in the small white chair as she held Richard's hand tight. She caressed it and held it up to her face. It was then that the air in the room felt cold, and then suddenly the room felt small as if it was closing in all around her.

"We're all alone, sweetheart," she said softly, running her fingers up and down the top of his hand with her love. Her eyes were not as strong as her heart, and as she looked at him with her dark spring-green eyes, a tear broke free from them and ran down the left side of her face.

Margaret stayed for an hour and made sure that the pillow was changed as per her request. With that, she headed home, but not before kissing Richard goodbye. Margaret then put Stacie's pillow on one of the white chairs, and walked out of the room, closing the door slowly behind her.

Sometime later, Stacie came to visit her father, and saw that the pillow she had brought for him sat on one of the chairs as if it had been tossed there with no care. She asked the nurses' station if anyone had been recently to visit Mr. Whiting. The two nurses on duty looked at each other and then back at Stacie, as if to tell her something. Instead, they just answered her question.

"Yes, his . . . wife," one of the nurses told her.

Stacie felt that her mother had taken her love and just tossed it away, that love she had given her father in the form of a pillow. Stacie then walked back to the room with rage and a heart full of pain. As she walked into the room and set eyes on her father's peaceful face, all the anger and pain slipped away.

"Hello, Daddy," she whispered in a soft voice as she sat down near him; her eyes began to swell with tears as she looked at him. She leaned forward to give him a kiss, and tears fell from her light blue eyes.

As she sat with him, she thought about what he wanted her to do a week before he had the accident. Richard wanted her to have a talk with her mother about what was going on between the two of them, because it was starting to get out of hand. It was at the point where Stacie would not go to the house for holiday dinners. Richard knew why, and so did Debbie. Richard had tried to talk to Margaret about the situation between her and Stacie, but Margaret always stopped him by telling him that he was only sticking up for his little girl, and that she could do her own talking if she wanted to.

Richard, at one point in time, had tried to figure out when it all started to go bad. He knew that Margaret was harder on Stacie then Debbie, but it hadn't always been that way. Margaret had always been fair with both girls when they were younger; it was not until they started getting older that he began to see a change, but even then he couldn't see it as a big change.

"I'll try and do what you have asked of me," she said to her father in a soft voice.

She sat back in the chair and thought about how nice it would be for her father to come back to a family that was as united, instead of one that was broken. He would be overjoyed to have two people he loved very much talking, instead of not talking. Stacie knew that it would be hard to talk to her mother about things, and that it was even harder to talk to a person that held something against you. Stacie never thought about it that much, and now that it was in her mind, it was difficult to push it out. Something inside of Stacie didn't care anymore why her own mother disliked her, but the only thing she could do now was just try and do what her father had asked of her, and hope that it would change things. She gave her father another kiss on the cheek and stood up.

"I love you, dad." She never grew out of calling him daddy, or dad. That was just her. That was what made Stacie stand out over her sister—that, and being breathtaking in her personality, and also in her nature. She left his bedside and as she did, she turned and looked around at the room. She noticed just how plain it was, and how something nice would bring it to life.

I'll bring a plant. That would be nice. It would put some color in this room, she thought to herself as she left.

2

Margaret laughed with friends and family at the lavish beach house as her hired maids in black-and-white uniforms served her and her guests a beautiful creamy pasta and salmon dish. There were finger foods as well, and champagne. For the kids that didn't like fish—which was all of them—there were homemade pizzas, chicken fingers, and fruit juice.

Sun shone down on everything and made the landscape glow; the rich pastel-green grass looked breathtaking beside all the small gardens around it, but the one garden that lit up the yard was the rose garden. Red, pink, and yellow roses made the yard look enchanted; the tulips, sunflowers, bluebells, and white roses were also enough to put you under a spell, and for most onlookers...it did.

All the trees looked alive as they moved in the sunlight and the light breeze; the water-colored blue sky held no clouds, and in a way, that light celeste blue sky helped the tall trees stand out a little more. It helped give the illusion that the trees were looking down at the flowers, and that the flowers were looking up at the trees.

Debbie walked past the flowers and looked at them all, she loved it when her mother got friends and family together for a special occasion, and this was the best thing by far that she had ever done for Richard. It was a birthday party, and even though he couldn't be here, everyone had come together for him. Margaret had even hired a professional photographer to capture this day just right, and to show Richard—in time—how everyone had gotten together just for him. She had even bought a giant birthday card, so that everyone could sign it.

Debbie walked near the bluebells, and touched one.

"Beautiful," a deep voice said.

She turned to see her boyfriend standing behind her with a drink.

"Thank you," she said taking the drink from him. "They are beautiful. I like them much more than the sunflowers," she told him.

"I wasn't talking about the flowers," he said, as he stepped back to look at her again. Debbie's ruby red knee-high dress showed off the true beauty of her figure and her long, wavy, medium-ash-brown hair cascaded over her shoulders with elegance.

"Stop. You're going to make me blush, Jason," she told him.

Jason was—in her eyes—a new boyfriend that would soon be a loving husband that would one day be a great father. After being together for almost a year, that plan was looking more and more likely. He was tall with a gorgeous face, walnut brown hair, and a strong build.

"My mother is waiting to see you. One day we will have to go and see my father and show him the photos of today," she told Jason as she pulled him by the hand.

Jason was a shy person, and he didn't want to act too nervous around her family. He looked at all the people at the party as he and Debbie walked towards the beach house; they were all dressed so nicely. All the ladies looked like they were out of some kind of fashion magazine. Everyone waved to them as they walked by, but Jason knew that it was Debbie the guests were really waving at. He felt a little uneasy around this crowd. Jason had growing up in a hard-working family, and at the age of thirty-one, he had done very well for himself. He started his own company just four years ago. It was an art company that did everything from web design to interior design. All the artwork was done from his office where he had three friends do most of the work. What he loved the most was working out at the job site and seeing the vision on the paper come to life before his eyes.

Margaret sat in the gazebo with three of her closest friends, watching Debbie and Jason walk across the yard.

"How has she been, Margaret?" Betty asked.

"Okay," Margaret said as she waved at Debbie.

"That's good," Betty said.

"That poor thing. Good thing you were there that day, Margaret," Isabel said.

"I know, but sometimes I don't think Debbie sees it like that. I don't even know how much of that day she remembers," Margaret said, looking over at Ivy who had held her tongue on the issue.

Margaret then turned back and called out to Debbie.

Debbie and Jason made their way over to her, and as they did, Jason didn't feel so nervous anymore. He suddenly felt relaxed as he looked at the lady who would one day be his mother-in-law. Margaret stood up and walked across the lawn and down the small stone set of stairs to greet them; her long blue summer dress moved gracefully with every shift of her body, like mist in a gentle breeze.

"Hello, sweetheart," she said, as she gave Debbie a hug and a kiss on the cheek.

"Mother, this is, Jason Green. Jason, this is my mother, Margaret Whiting," Debbie said as she stepped back.

"It's a pleasure to meet you, Jason," Margaret said reaching out to shake his hand.

"It's a pleasure to meet you as well," Jason replied as he shook her hand.

"So, Jason, what do you think of the beach?" Margaret asked him, waving her hand through the air.

"It's beautiful," he said, as he looked around. Some of the guests were looking back at him, and they looked different this time, like mannequins in a store window: all dolled-up and lifeless inside.

"It was left to me after my mother passed on. I love it here. I come down to the beach as much as I can. Isn't that right, dear?" Margaret said, turning to Debbie. It was then that Margaret could see that Jason was looking at three men in black suits. "Don't mind them, love. They think they own the world. Debbie, you should show Jason around," she then said, smiling at him. Jason smiled back.

"That would be nice," Jason, said, "I would really like to see the rest of the beach."

"It's settled then. Debbie will show you around, and I'll see you both a little later. By the way, Debbie, your sister should be here. Have you seen her yet?" Margaret asked, looking around.

"No," Debbie said.

"Okay. I'll see you two in a little bit," Margaret said as she walked away, calling out to one of her friends.

Debbie and Jason walked towards the beach house, and as they did, Jason looked over at the hill and the tall trees. He could see a stone staircase that went all the way to the top of the hill.

"Where do those stairs lead?" Jason inquired.

"Just to a side street," Debbie told him as they walked into the house.

When they entered the house Debbie spotted Stacie talking to their cousin, Vincent. Vincent didn't talk long, and after he left Debbie and Jason walked up to Stacie. She turned and smiled.

"Hello, sis," she said to Debbie.

"Hello, Stacie. I love your dress," Debbie said. Stacie was wearing a long baby blue dress with white lace gloves.

"I'd like you to meet my boyfriend, Jason."

"Hello," she said. Stacie was too shy to shake anyone's hand when she didn't know them; the only time she really did was when she had to through work, but she was usually around the same people, and to her that was like her own little family.

"Hello. It's nice to meet you," Jason said, reaching out to shake her hand, but it was met with coldness.

Jason put his hand back down to the side, and just looked at her.

"Don't let it get to you, Jason. Stacie doesn't like shaking hands," Debbie said as she gave her sister a little smirk. Stacie then reached out her hand and looked at Jason. They shook hands and said hello again as they both smiled at each other. It was then and only at that moment that Jason saw how beautiful she was. He looked deep into her eyes as she looked at him and then over at Debbie.

"There, you see. I can shake hands," Stacie said. "Have I ever told you how much I love having a big sister?" Stacie said, rolling her eyes.

"Yes. Yes you have," Debbie replied as they both laughed over the playful teasing.

"Sorry, Jason, we do that sometimes to each other. It's a sister thing," Debbie told him.

Jason just stood there and smiled within the moment.

"Stacie, mom was asking about you. She is in the gazebo," Debbie told her.

"Okay, I have to talk to her anyhow, but I don't know if this is the right place, or the right time," Stacie could hear what her voice was saying, but her mind couldn't comprehend it.

"Stacie, this is father's birthday party, whether he is here or not. Save it for another time," Debbie told her.

"Okay. I'll just go and say hello," Stacie said.

Stacie said goodbye to Jason and Debbie, and went off to see her mother. Debbie and Jason made their way into the living room; the room was very large, and it made Jason feel small. He walked over to the bay window and could see all the guests outside; he could also see Stacie walking across the grass, and it was then that she turned towards the window and waved at him. Jason waved back with no control over his body or his feelings. It was hard not to see the beauty in Stacie. Her light blue eyes and long flowing blonde hair were hard to turn away from.

"Jason!" Debbie called out to him, snapping him out of his daze. "Come and look at my mother's candlestick-holder collection," she said.

Jason looked out the window one last time before heading over to Debbie, but Stacie had gone. Jason couldn't believe how many different candlestick holders there were. Debbie told him that it was her grandmother who had started the collection, and that her mother felt she had to keep it going after her grandmother died. There were holders from all over the world; most of them were Victorian-style. Jason saw three candleholders that were monkeys. One was tall––ten inches, and had its hands over its ears. Then there was one that was seven inches high, and it had its hands over his mouth. The last one was about four inches tall and it had its hands over its eyes.

"Hear no evil. Speak no evil. See no evil," Jason said under his breath.

"What?" Debbie asked.

"The three monkeys. The candlestick holders," Jason said as he pointed at them.

"Oh, I haven't seen them before. They must be old," she said.

"How can you tell?" Jason asked.

"See how there's candles in the front of them?"

"Yes," he replied.

"Well, my grandmother always put the newer ones up in front; the older ones sat in the back," she told him.

"I see," Jason said.

Near the candlestick holders at the end of the table stood two old pictures in gold and silver frames; they gleamed in the sunlight streaming into the room through the large bay window. It almost made the two old photos look lost in time, or lost in the bright light that helped the pictures look faded and almost transparent.

"That's my mom and my aunt Peg," Debbie told him.

Jason didn't see it at first, but as he looked a little closer he could see that her aunt Peg looked just like Margaret. He then picked up the picture in the gold frame and held it up to his face so that it was out of the light that obscured the image. When he'd had a good look, he put it back down and turned to Debbie.

"Your mother and aunt are twins?"

"Yes," she said with a big grin. "It took you that long to see that? What I mean is, I know the photo is a good twenty-years old, but they're not that old," Debbie said.

"Is your aunt here today?" Jason asked.

"No, she went missing when Stacie and I were very young," she told him.

"I'm sorry."

"It's okay. It was so long ago, yet I still remember little things about her," Debbie said as she picked up the next picture. It was a photo of her mother and father. Her mother was sitting at a table signing the marriage license, and her father stood behind her with his right hand on her shoulder. Debbie could see that her mother was holding his hand as she signed the marriage license, and to her that simple sign of love between two people was all that mattered; she could only hope that she and Jason would share that same kind of love one day.

Debbie told Jason how much she and her sister loved to come up here as children, and how they would go swimming in the ocean no matter how cold it was. There was a time when their mother and aunt Peg would both stand on the shoreline and watch them swim. Debbie could remember even back then that it was so hard to tell who was who unless they had on something different, but their mother always had on one thing that was different.

"A gold necklace," Debbie told Jason. "It was a Christmas gift from me and Stacie when we were young. Dad bought it, but you know. It was from us—even though she knew it wasn't—and she loved it just the same. Then one day I noticed that she wasn't wearing it, and I never saw it again," she told Jason.

"Did you ever ask her about it? Jason asked.

"No, Stacie was the one that asked her. Stacie was only young, around six or seven, I'm not even sure how young she was at the time, but I remember... I remember."

"What?" Jason asked as he looked into her eyes. She seemed to be lost in the past.

"Mother yelled at Stacie for asking her about it, but it was more than that, my father told me when I was a little older. He told me that Stacie had pulled on the neckline of her dress to see if she was wearing the gold chain, and then asked her about it. Father told me that mother got mad at Stacie because her sister had bought her that dress. Stacie was too young to understand, and now that she is older, she and mother have had a hard time seeing eye-to-eye," she said, looking at him.

Jason was just about to open his mouth when he heard someone call out to Debbie. It was Stacie, and as she walked over to them, Jason couldn't help but examine her body and the way she moved it as she approached. He couldn't lie to himself; he liked the way she moved, and found her irresistible and breathtaking.

"There you are. Mom wishes to speak with you immediately," Stacie said in a stuck-up, snobbish tone of voice, mimicking their mother.

"Is that how she said it? Or are you just trying to get her in a bad mood?" Debbie asked as she walked past her.

Stacie just stood there for a minute and then turned and called out to Debbie. "I'm sorry, sis." Stacie said, not taking her apology serious as Debbie looked back at her.

"Okay, thank you, Stacie. I'll be back in a minute, Jason," Debbie said with a grin as she continued walking down the small hill towards the gazebo.

Jason looked at Stacie, and Stacie looked at him. She couldn't begin to think of what Jason was thinking, and if his thoughts were of her, or of how she had just acted in front of him.

"Sorry about that, I was just telling her what was told to me," Stacie said.

"Your mother said it just like that?" Jason asked Stacie.

"Yes, mom and I have something to talk about, and plus, that's how mom is."

Jason didn't know what to say, but a part of him wanted to comfort her. Her beauty was too much for him—or any man, for that matter — to walk away from. Jason found that he was now within that realm. He just looked at her, but didn't say anything, and was unable to move or walk away.

"You, okay?" Stacie asked, as she saw him looking at her blankly.

"Yes," he said still holding her gaze.

She smiled at him in the same way she had no more than half an hour ago. She could tell that Jason had eyes for her, but he was with someone she loved with all her heart, even though she never showed it all the time. Debbie was dear to Stacie's heart, and would always be.

Debbie came back to the house and walked over to Stacie and Jason, who were talking in the living room.

"So, what are you two talking about?" Debbie asked, taking Jason by the arm in a loving way.

"Jason was just telling me all about his business," Stacie told her, and then asked, "How did it go with mom? What did she want?"

"Nothing, really. Just wanted to ask me something," Debbie said as if she was going over the conversation in her mind. There was something in her eyes, and Stacie could see it. "She also asked me to tell you that everyone is going to get together down by the boat-dock in about an hour for a group photo."

"That will look nice on the card," Stacie said as she looked out the window towards the beach.

They talked a little longer, and the more they did, the more Jason saw just how close they were. Jason could only wish that he and his brother could be that close, but they had drifted apart since their father passed away.

Time passed quickly, and before they all knew it, they were down by the beach on the boat-dock that reached out like an arm into the ocean. Most of the people stood on the beach; they were raising their champagne glasses and singing happy birthday.

"Can I have everyone say 'Happy Birthday, Richard,' at once? Nice and loud and all together?" the photographer asked.

Everyone started to count: "one, two, and three," and then everyone yelled out, "Happy Birthday, Richard!"

After the photo was taken, Margaret asked if everyone would sign the giant birthday card. Margaret found it hard to watch her friends and family walk up to the card and write their name and a little message of their love for him. Most people just wrote: "Get Well," "We Love You," and "Come Home Soon."

Everyone stayed late until the night started to creep in from the east and slowly cover the landscape in darkness. One by one, family and friends said goodbye to Margaret, and she thanked them for coming. Margaret was very grateful for their attendance despite Richard's absence. Everyone knew how hard she had worked to set it all up months ago; it was a good way for the family to be together in this hard time.

As soon as they got home, Debbie asked Jason what he felt about her family, and even though he could hear her, he could only think of meeting one person at that party. He saw Stacie's face floating in his mind when he closed his eyes. Her long blonde hair and her blue eyes seemed so real in his mind that it made his voice fall silent in the back of his throat. As she waited, watching him, he couldn't find any words to answer Debbie.

"Well, what did you think of them?"

"They're very nice," he said, picking up an iced tea he'd left on the coffee table before they left for the party, and taking a sip; it was as warm as the summer night.

"That's good. I'm glad you like them," she said, smiling at him.

Jason asked her about her mother. He thought she was kind when she'd told him not to worry about the men who were looking at him.

"My mother is a good person. She's just looking out for you, because we are together, and maybe one day you will be part of the family," she told him as she leaned on the fridge.

"I know she is a good person, honey, but I don't think your sister sees it that way."

"My sister? First of all: don't believe everything that Stacie tells you about mother," she said, pushing herself away from the fridge.

"Okay, if you say so," Jason said looking down at his iced tea with hurt on his face, he then turned and walked out onto the back deck. Debbie thought to herself for a moment and then went out to him. She stood at the door and just watched him looking up at the night sky. She walked up behind Jason and wrapped her arms around him.

"I love you," she said, resting her head on his back.

"I love you too," he told her.

"I shouldn't have said that about, Stacie," she said.

"It's okay," Jason said placing his hands on top of hers.

"I know that mother loves us both, but something happened between her and Stacie, and ever since then, mother somewhat disliked her; something more than just pulling on her dress had to have happened. It's something I can't quite figure out," she said looking into his eyes. "I have seen things that have always made me wonder, but in the end, I just let it go. I feel that she has always loved her deep down, but Stacie feels that our mother's love is gone. Mother talks down to her a lot, and puts me before her all the time. Stacie and father are the only two people in the family who work, for God's sake; the rest of us are just doing whatever we want. Father has always wanted to keep the company going, because that was the one thing that made him what he is today, and Stacie has always wanted to be a model. I can still remember when Stacie would go into mother's room and get all dolled-up, and that was when mother would get really mad at her. She would yell at her and pull her out of the room, but that didn't stop Stacie. Stacie would be right back in there the next day putting on pearls, shiny dresses, and black high heels that wouldn't fit her for another ten years." Debbie gave him a kiss and then told him that she was getting tired. He knew that she just didn't want to talk about things anymore, and that was okay with him. After all, she was the one that brought it up, so she had all the say in not wanting to take it any further.

Jason couldn't pull himself away from the starlit night sky, and he found it equally difficult to pull himself away from his own thoughts of Stacie.

What was it that pulled his heart to her? What was it that pulled his mind to her? What created the pull to be by her side, and the desire to embrace her in his arms, and the need to hold her close to his soul?

Soon his gaze fell to the treetops, and then to the pool that lay under them. It was then that a cold chill came over him—coldness sank into his bones as if it was a cold winter's night—and he knew that his thoughts were wrong. He knew that he couldn't be with her. He also knew that his heart wanted her; it was a feeling he couldn't ignore.

Debbie phoned her mother the next day to ask her if she would like to have lunch with her and Jason at the Italian restaurant near the mall. Debbie thought that this would be a good time for Jason and her mother to get to know each other a little better. Margaret was delighted that Debbie had called to ask her to lunch. She also agreed that it was a good chance for her and Jason to get to know each other and to talk without a lot of people around. Debbie told her that she would make it for Saturday when Jason was free from work. Debbie thought that Jason would be a little upset that she had made reservations without asking him beforehand, but he was fine with it. Jason told her that he was thinking the same thing, and that it would be nice for them to get to know each other a little better over lunch. Debbie was so happy to hear those words come out of his mouth.

Saturday came and Debbie and Jason arrived at the restaurant fifteen minutes early. Margaret was already inside waiting for them; there was even a drink already in front of her. Margaret waved to them as they walked towards the table. She was seated in the middle of the very large room that featured an old oil painting hanging high on the wall. Jason had never been in a restaurant like this before; its size was overwhelming to any newcomer.

"Hello, mother," Debbie said as Jason pulled out one of the fancy solid wood chairs for Debbie. It felt heavy and the carmine-red leather cushions held a rich shine in the light, almost like the color of fire over gold. Jason then said hello to Margaret and asked how she was before he himself sat down.

"I'm just fine, dear. How about yourself?" Margaret asked as she smiled at him.

"I'm fine," Jason said as Debbie gestured for the waiter.

They eat, drank, and talked into the afternoon. Jason was starting to get a feel for this lady who sat across from him. Yet there was something that told him to look past that sweet face, and past the make-up that helped obscure her real age; Jason just couldn't unravel that something about her left him suspicious.

Jason was good at reading people—his friends had always told him—and he was very good at observing every little thing about what people did or said; after all, he was an artist, and attention to detail was one of his strong suits.

They relaxed after their meal and talked some more. Debbie got a call on her cell phone and as it rang and rang, the talking between them was suspended. It took Debbie a minute or two to answer it, and when she did, she excused herself so that Jason and her mother could continue talking without interruption.

Margaret watched Debbie walk away as Jason talked on; Jason was watching Margaret's eyes follow Debbie right into the lobby. He noticed that Margaret only looked away once Debbie had reached the bench near the entrance. Margaret then turned to Jason and asked him how he felt about Debbie. Jason felt that uneasy feeling return to him, and at first all he could do was look at her a little puzzled by her question. Clouding his mind was the thought of Stacie, who he had only met once.

"Debbie is everything to me. She is the one person I want to be with for the rest of my life. That is how I feel even though it has not quite been a year yet. It's hard for me to meet people, so I'm very happy that I have met Debbie," he explained.

"I see. That's nice; she is a very nice girl who deserves to be with someone that will love her for who she is. So, did you enjoy yourself yesterday at the beach house?" Margaret asked.

"Yes," Jason said, "it was so nice." He glanced over to see if Debbie was on her way back to the table; he was feeling uneasy and couldn't take much more. He felt that Margaret was digging for something that wasn't there. Jason looked back at Margaret to see her grinning at him.

"So, did, Debbie introduce you to her sister yesterday?" Margaret asked him with inquisitive eyes.

"Yes," he replied slowly as he could tell that she was looking deep into his weak soul.

"She is beautiful, isn't she? What do you think of her?" Margaret asked as if she knew how his heart felt.

"She . . ."

"Hello, dear," Margaret said suddenly cutting Jason off as Debbie returned.

Debbie sat down and gave Jason a kiss on the side of the cheek. Jason asked if everything was alright, and as he did, Margaret waved the waiter over to the table.

"Everything is fine. That was just Stacie," Debbie said.

Margaret then sighed and asked what she wanted.

"She wanted to know if we were going to the hospital sometime today. She is already there, so I told her that we may go after we are done are lunch," Debbie told her mother.

Margaret said that would be fine, but a look of uncertainty covered her face like a mask. In her mind, she had just been there and it pained her to see her husband incapacitated in a hospital bed.

I should be there. I should be by his side, but it's hard for me to go. Yet if I don't go, he may wake up and I will not be there. It would be Stacie that he'd see first. It would be her that calls to her daddy, instead of his wife calling to him, she thought as she got up out of her chair.

"Are you okay, Mother? If you don't feel like going, we don't have to."

"Yes, I do have to!" Margaret snapped at Debbie. "I'm sorry dear, but I hate to see him like that. I really love him so, and I just want him to come back to us. I was just there the other day, and I didn't think that I would have to go back this soon. When I'm not there I like to think of all the good times we have had growing old together, that's all," she told Debbie and Jason.

Debbie didn't say anything as they left the restaurant, but she knew that her mother hated seeing him like that, and for Debbie it was just as hard. Debbie looked at her mother and then held her hand to comfort her. She also knew that Margaret preferred seeing her husband to seeing her estranged daughter, Stacie, and Debbie thought that was what was really holding Margaret back from visiting the hospital.

3

Margaret's found herself stepping back into that cold white room; with her eyes slightly closed, it felt like she was gliding, as if she were drifting in a dream. Like any dream, it ended as her eyes opened. Margaret was hoping for some good news today, maybe a little change, but there was nothing new with Richard. Richard was still in the same state that he had been the last time she came to see him—lifeless and lost to the family that was his world. Margaret would stay with him until their worlds were as one again. She showed her undying love for him with a kiss on his soft lips; she knew that the man she loved was inside that slumbering body, and that he would feel her warm kiss and know that she was by his side. Margaret looked at Debbie with hope in her eyes, but her hope was growing dull with each passing week and little improvement for Richard.

"Are you okay, Mother?" Debbie asked.

"Yes, dear," she replied.

Debbie took in the room, lifeless as a blank canvas except for a plant and a card that read: "Get well, Dad." Debbie knew that Stacie had brought it. It was the kind of thing Stacie would do. Debbie's focus was broken by the sound of Margaret's low sobbing. Debbie went over to her and held her mother in her arms. Both women were overcome with emotion as they looked down at the man who meant so much to them. Debbie helped her mother walk over to an armchair. She was surprised at how difficult it was to help her mother; it felt as if she was helping an old lady she didn't know cross the street. When Margaret sat down she seemed a little unsteady.

"Mother, do you want me and Jason to take you home?" Debbie asked.

"No, I want to stay a little longer," she said, gazing at Richard.

"Are you sure?" Debbie asked, knowing that she was not feeling well.

"I'll be fine, dear," Margaret told her, "I'm just tired."

Debbie asked her if she wanted a coffee, suggesting that it may be just what she needed. Debbie suddenly wondered where Stacie could have gone.

"That would be nice, I would like that," Margaret said.

"I'll get them, Debbie," Jason offered, "You stay here with your mother. How do you like your coffee?" Jason asked Margaret.

"Two cream, one sugar, dear," she told him, giving him a soft, warm smile.

"Thank you, sweetheart," Debbie said with loving eyes and caressed Jason's shoulder with tenderness. Jason grabbed her hand and kissed it softly, holding her gaze, then said, "Coffees, coming right up," and excused himself. Jason knew what her eyes were really saying as he peered beyond that loving look.

"I love you. I love you with all my heart."

Jason made his way down to the small food court, and waited in a line that he imagined never shrank. Some of the faces in the line looked as long as the line itself, yet he didn't mind because it gave him a little more time to think of the look in Debbie's eyes. Drifting away in his thoughts, Jason could almost hear her voice calling out to him, but it was not her voice, nor was it was in his mind. The voice that pushed its way into his mind was as sweet as the one that he was imagining. Jason shook his head slightly to break free from his Debbie trance, and as he turned around, he came face to face with someone that he thought was much more beautiful.

"Hello, Jason. Where's Debbie?" Stacie asked, as Jason stared at her, stunned.

"Hello, Stacie. Debbie and your mother are already in the room," he replied, still holding his gaze on her. Jason was locked in a trace as they talked casually. She asked if her mother had seen the iris plant in the room.

"I'm not sure, but I think Debbie saw it. I like it. It p—"

"Puts some life into that room, and some color," she said interrupting him, and giving him a grin.

"You took the words right out of my mouth," Jason told her.

Jason was up next in line, and he couldn't believe how fast the line had shrunk. Jason offered to buy for Stacie, but she wouldn't have it. Jason then ordered the coffees for Debbie and Margaret, and stood off to the side to wait. He couldn't help but stare at this beautiful person that was in his thoughts and in his world, and as he looked on, she turned to him and smiled. She'd caught him looking. Jason's heart raced as Stacie smirked at him. Stacie got her coffee and donut and walked over to Jason.

"Ready to head upstairs?" Jason asked, as she got closer to him.

"Yes, but first let me eat my donut. Would you like half? I can't eat the whole thing," she told him as she broke it in two.

"What do you mean, you can't eat the whole thing?" Jason asked.

"Well, you know what my occupation is, right?"

"Yes," he said.

"Well, I can't eat the whole thing," she told him again, as she handed him half of the donut with a smile.

"I don't think that a little donut is going to change the way you look; a dozen donuts wouldn't do anything to your beauty or your figure," he said turning away from her. It just slipped out, and it sounded corny. Jason felt embarrassed by his own words.

"Thank you," she said.

"I'm sorry for what I just said. I—"

"It's okay," she told him, "just never say things like that again," Stacie told him, with a disarming grin. There was a part of him that could tell she was joking with him, but the other part of him didn't know for sure.

The elevator doors opened and as they squeezed in together, Jason's heart raced a little faster then before; it felt small because they were not alone. There were two doctors in there with them as they made their way to the fourth floor.

"Jason," Stacie softly called to him, "I was just pulling your leg, you know," she told him, looking into his eyes.

"I know," he said with a big smile, and he was relieved.

On the second floor a nurse came on, and then a woman with a large handbag.

"It's a full-house in here," one of the doctors commented as the doors closed.

As they reached the fourth floor, Jason and Stacie moved closer to the doors, but when they opened more people were trying to get on. Jason was able to get out of that metal box, but Stacie had a hard time getting past an old man.

"I'm sorry," he said to Stacie as he let her pass, "I didn't think you two were together at first. I'm sorry for keeping your wife from you, Sir," that old man said, looking over at Jason.

"That's, okay," Jason replied, giving the old man a little wave. Stacie walked over to Jason, who was holding back his laughter until the elevator doors closed.

"What is it? What is so amusing?" Stacie asked him.

"That old man thought that he was keeping my wife from me. I was a little worried for a moment, I thought I was going to lose you forever," he said as he let out his uncontainable laughter.

"It's not that funny," she said, catching sight of their blurred reflections in the gray metal elevator doors. Stacie turned so that Jason couldn't see her funny, embarrassed grin.

"I'm sorry, but it was funny, if you were on the right side of the door," he said, and she flashed him a grin.

"Well, I was on the side that wasn't so funny," she replied as they walked down the hall and past the nurses' station to the room.

Jason was about to ask Stacie about her mother. It was on the tip of his tongue, but he held back his words. He had just met her no more then two days ago, and he didn't want to make the same mistake with her as he had with Debbie the other night.

Jason and Stacie looked as each other one last time before they entered the room; it was more like a glance that meant goodbye, but not forever. When they walked into the room all heads turned—all but Richard's—and for a minute, no one spoke.

"Hello, honey. Here you go," Jason, said as he handed Debbie her coffee, and then he handed Margaret hers.

"Thank you, Jason," Margaret said, eyeing Stacie.

"Thank you, sweetheart," Debbie then said.

"You're welcome," he replied.

Debbie and Margaret both said hello to Stacie as they opened their coffees. Debbie asked her where she had gone. Stacie told her that she had to use the restroom and that she'd gone down to the food court to get a coffee, when she ran into Jason.

Margaret asked if Stacie talked to Jason at the Tim Horton's, or if she just stood there and said nothing. Margaret looked up at Jason to see if his face revealed anything to her. Stacie didn't know what to say; she knew that she wanted to avoid any argument with Margaret. This was not the place for the two of them to get into it, and Stacie felt strongly about it in her heart.

Stacie wished that her father would come out of his coma. If he could, she knew that he would say something to Margaret. He always tried to keep the peace in the family when there was something wrong.

Jason stepped forward and told Margaret that Stacie was nice to him the whole time in line, and that she talked to him as they waited. "She was very sociable," he assured Margaret.

"She did?" Margaret replied in a churlish tone of voice, looking down at Stacie.

"Mom, stop," Debbie spoke out. Stacie had her head down and slowly lifted it to take a sip of her cappuccino when Debbie stood up for her.

"It's okay, Debbie. I'm leaving now. I got here very early and I'm a little tired," Stacie said as she looked towards her mother with steely eyes. Stacie gave her father a kiss on his forehead and then turned and walked out of the room.

Debbie asked her mother why she had questioned Stacie, and insisted there was no need for it. Margaret told her that she didn't mean anything by it, and that she should know by now that her sister has always been touchy.

"She is too shy," Margaret said. "You know how she can get, Debbie, and if Jason is going to be a part of this family, people are going to have to warm up to him."

Jason assured Margaret that Stacie hadn't just stood there, but that she had spoken to him as a friend. Jason didn't add that he had said some things that were on the edge of flirting. He also made it clear that she had talked to him at the beach house, so there was no need for Margaret to think that her daughter was being rude towards him.

"She'll get over it as time goes on," Margaret said.

"Will, she?" Jason commented.

Margaret slowly looked up at Jason, her face cold in a way he had never seen before; it was as if she could tell that he had eyes for Stacie just by the way he had said those two little words; he was reminded of the intensity of her gaze on him in the restaurant. Margaret looked down at her hands and told him that she would.

"She'll forget about this day; unlike other days," Margaret muttered as she stood up and turned to the window.

Debbie watched her mother, knowing full well that she was not really thinking about how her words had made Stacie feel. Debbie told her mother she should go talk to Stacie before it was too late. Margaret grabbed Debbie's hand and told her that it was already too late, and that she could not take back what she had just said.

Debbie knew that she would have to go and talk to Stacie eventually. She didn't want to, but if her mother couldn't bring herself to do it, then she would. Debbie and Jason hurried out of the room in hopes that they would catch up with Stacie before she left the hospital. Debbie could see her leaning up against the wall waiting for the elevator, and feared that if she didn't call out to her, Stacie would just get on it as soon as the doors opened––even if she saw Debbie at the end of the hall.

"Stacie!" Debbie called out to her. Stacie's head turned to catch Debbie and Jason drawing near. Jason could see the hurt in Stacie's face, and his heart went out to her without anyone knowing it. Jason couldn't imagine what it would be like to have a mother who didn't give a damn about you, yet cared so deeply for your sibling.

"I don't feel like talking right now, Debbie," Stacie said, concealing her eyes from them, and Debbie and Jason knew why. Debbie also knew that Stacie had a hard time controlling her emotions when someone really hurt her. The one person who could hurt Stacie better then anyone was their mother. What Margaret had said was nothing, but it was everything to Stacie. Everything that was going on between them entwined with those words. It was hard for her not to let it dig deep and pierce her heart like a knife.

"Will, you at least call me tonight? Please," Debbie pleaded as the elevator doors opened.

"Okay," Stacie said before the doors closed between them.

"Do you really think she'll call?" Jason asked.

"I don't know," Debbie said knowing that when things got to Stacie it took some time for her to get over them.

Jason remarked that Margaret might not know Stacie as well as she thinks she does. Debbie turned and spoke up for her mother in a way that Jason had never seen before.

"What are you talking about? She is our mother. Who else is going to know us better then her?" Debbie's face almost looked like Stacie's, full of hurt. "Jason, when it comes to my mother and sister, please stay out of it," she told him.

"Okay," he agreed, hugging her tightly, and quickly kissing her ruby red lips. He knew that Debbie couldn't have said it nicer, but she was right no matter how it sounded. He had just met her sister and mother, and more time would have to go by before he would have any say in this family. Jason knew that this problem between Margaret and Stacie had been going on for years; he only knew this because Debbie had told him. Debbie was clear that she did not want any help from him, but his intentions were good. In a way, it was hard to sit back and watch Debbie go though this on her own, but if she was sure of what she wanted, then he would stand by her decision.

They walked back to the room hand-in-hand, and Debbie pondered what she was going to tell her mother. It would do no good to tell her how much she had hurt Stacie, because she would probably just turn her nose up to it. As she thought about it a little more, Debbie knew that the best thing would be to say nothing. Debbie knew she had to let go and allow it to pass by like a storm in the darkness of the night.

Margaret walked out of the room and saw Debbie and Jason walking past that nurses' station. They were at the hospital so often that station was starting to become part of their lives. Margaret was carrying a large handbag with a blanket in it. She had brought it for Richard a few days ago, and now she was going to take it home and wash it. Debbie and Jason rushed up to Margaret and asked why she was leaving so soon. All Margaret could do was look Debbie in the eye as if to say: *You know damn well why.*

"I had a lovely day. Thank you both for lunch, but it has been a long day. I have to clean your father's blanket. It's a good thing I brought two the other day, because I didn't think I would be back this soon," Margaret said holding on tightly to the handbag. Jason could see that she had the blanket from the bed in her bag, but what he didn't see was the way she was watching him as Debbie talked to her.

"Mother? Mother!" Debbie called out to her even though she was standing right next to her. Margaret was fixated on Jason eyeing her handbag. She had drifted off into a world where she could not hear anything but her own thoughts. She was trying to piece together what Jason was looking at.

Debbie asked her mother if she was okay; it had been twice now in two days that she had asked her mother this question. Debbie was a little worried; Margaret had never acted like this before. Debbie knew that she was going through a lot, but she seemed to be taking her stress out on people—innocent people like that little petite nurse who was only doing her job—like Stacie, who had not said anything deserving the comments that came out of Margaret's mouth. Debbie knew that there was something wrong with the two of them, and it was getting worse.

Debbie and Jason said goodbye to Margaret. Debbie noticed that Margaret didn't even ask what was said between her and Stacie; in a way she was not surprised. Debbie and Jason went into see Richard before they headed home themselves. Debbie gave her father a kiss and touched his head lovingly. Just as Jason was about to close the door on their way out, he noticed that the small iris plant Stacie had brought was gone from the nightstand. He glanced at Debbie and decided against bringing up the disappearance of the plant.

"We should hurry and get home. I have things to do, and I don't want to miss Stacie's call," Debbie said as she put her arm around Jason. Her eyes were wet, and even though she didn't say it, he could tell that she wanted her father back. All he could do was hold her tight as they walked back towards the elevator.

4

Debbie's soft lips kissed the side of Jason's neck, and her teeth gently pulled at his earlobe. He grabbed her firm buttocks and pulled her closer towards him. Jason lifted her up, and she wrapped her legs around him; her rose petal, silk panties pressed up against Jason's exposed penis, and the body heat from within those silky panties drove Jason to the edge of pleasure.

It was not long before they both fell into the world of ecstasy. When Debbie took Jason's fully erect penis deep into her, Jason fell into two worlds. Debbie sat up on him as he sprawled on the bed, and she began to make love to him, pushing him into that second world of his dreams; the world Jason wanted was shared with the one person he couldn't be with, the one person deep inside his thoughts.

Stacie, he thought, but he dare not speak her name. Jason suddenly kissed Debbie passionately, sitting up and holding her in his arms. He ran his fingers though her hair and in his different world her hair was blond and her eyes were sky blue. Debbie gasped as she pushed down on him, digging her glossy fingernails into his back; simply thinking of Stacie pushed Jason to the pinnacle of climax; he could no longer control his body. Debbie also reached climax, but felt that it was too soon for her liking. As they lay in bed still holding onto one another and talking softly, it felt like it was the first time with each other. She felt satisfied, but wished that it could have lasted longer. She wondered what it was that she had done to suddenly make him so aroused.

"Wow," she said, throwing her head back into the pillow as she looked up at the ceiling and the dim lights that hung there; they were so dim that their naked bodies were almost in complete darkness. "Where did that come from?" Debbie asked, turning towards him; Jason was also looking up at the dim lights.

"I don't know. It was just...in me, I guess," he told her, sounding unsure. He felt that Debbie was asking only to find out something, as if she was probing his mind.

She started to rub his chest and kissed his shoulder, and before he could turn to give her a kiss, she told him that she was sorry about the day and what she had said at the hospital. She knew that he was only trying to help, but at the time she couldn't see it. Jason could only hold her and tell her that she didn't have to apologize. He explained that he understood how she most have felt knowing that two people she cares about are unwilling to see eye-to-eye. Debbie held him tight after hearing him say that.

Jason slid out of bed and walked over to the other side. He reached out his hand and asked Debbie if she would like to accompany him to the shower; she smiled at him and took his hand, and as she stood up she kissed him with the same passion she had before. They made their way into the washroom and closed the door. Debbie pulled Jason into the shower, and, under the hot water, Jason took hold of her from behind with the same raw passion that had came over him earlier. This time he was present with Debbie and not the person who was in his thoughts.

Her long brown hair clung to her body as they made love in the steam-filled shower, and as they did, Jason's hands cupped her wet breasts and squeezed them.

"Debbie," he said in a voice that was almost a whisper. He squeezed her breast tighter, and kissed her on the cheek. She knew that Jason was begging for her moist lips, and so she turned and kissed him slowly.

Back in bed, both laid in comfort and were fully satisfied. Debbie and Jason talked as they both slowly started to get tired. Jason looked at her and then turned away.

"What is it?" Debbie asked.

Jason didn't want to say anything, but there was something on his mind, and he needed to get it off his chest.

"Jason, what is it?"

"Can I ask you something without you getting upset?"

"Yes," she says with an odd feeling inside of her, as if she already knew what he was going to ask.

"It's about your mother," he said.

"Okay, what about her?"

"She asked me something today that seemed odd to me. She asked me right after she had asked me how I felt about you," Jason began to tell her, but felt a little out of place after making love to her.

Debbie looked at him with eyes that were telling him to stop, but she had not spoken any words. Jason told her that she had asked him something about Stacie just before she returned to the table. Debbie jumped up and looked at the clock as soon as she heard Stacie's name.

She hasn't called yet, and it's already past ten, she thought.

"What is it, Debbie?" Jason asked, fearing it was something he had said.

"It's nothing," she told him.

She asked him what it was her mother had said to him, and he told her that she had asked him if he thought Stacie was beautiful.

"It was so out of the ordinary," he said, looking at her.

Jason asked Debbie why her mother would ask him something like that. Debbie told Jason that her mother has always looked out for her, and that maybe she just thought that he liked Stacie more than her.

"If your mother thinks that way, then maybe she should have been invited over tonight for the last two times we made love. That would change her way of thinking," Jason replied with a grin.

"Jason! Debbie said in a shocked voice. She slapped him playfully on his shoulder.

"I don't mean it. You know that. I'm just saying, she shouldn't think that way, and she shouldn't ask me things like that," he said.

"I know you didn't mean it, but I don't want to hear about my mother watching us go at it like a couple of animals," she told him. Giving him a grin of her own.

It was right then that the phone began to ring, and Debbie jumped to her feet to answer it. She picked it up and said hello. On the other end was a low voice of sadness that was her sister, and through the tears, Stacie asked Debbie why their mother hated her. Debbie's world of pleasure crumbled, and Debbie's mind was violently pushed back into the reality of her life with her family.

Stacie calmed down a little and started talking to Debbie with a soothing voice, but Debbie knew her sister all too well. Stacie was calming herself for Debbie, because Stacie in turn knew Debbie's past.

"You know how she is, and that world that she lives in. You can't let her get to you," Debbie told her. Debbie told Stacie that she had to start coming to the house for dinners more often, so that when father came back home it won't feel so odd.

"I thought I knew her. When Dad comes home I will come over for dinner, but only when Dad comes back home, because I know that mom will never look at me like a daughter," Stacie said. Stacie told Debbie that she would only go and see Dad in the hospital as long as Mom was not there, and that it would be better that way. Debbie asked Stacie how she would even know when Mother was at the hospital, and before Stacie could answer, Debbie knew that it would be up to her to let Stacie know.

"I would like it if you could let me know when Mom is planning to go see Dad; she tells you everything, and she will never question why you are asking her. Please…for me," Stacie asked with sorrow in her voice.

"Okay, but I'm only doing this for you because I love you. You have to promise me that you are going to try to figure out how to patch things up with her before Father comes home," Debbie explained to her.

Stacie thanked her. She felt a warm flow of relief consume her body. Stacie told Debbie that Jason was nice to her in the food court when she was talking to him. Stacie didn't understand why their mother would say that she wasn't being nice when she wasn't even there. Stacie told Debbie that it was better not to even talk to her, and Debbie told her that that would not change anything. Debbie knew that it was probably hopeless—like trying to talk to fading watercolored faces on a dirty white wall—yet not talking to her would not solve anything for sure.

Jason could hear Debbie talking to Stacie from the bathroom where he had gone when Debbie answered the phone. When he heard his name ringing in his ears, he knew that Stacie had mentioned him in some way or another. He thought of her as he came back into the bedroom. He rolled back into bed and onto his side, and as he did, Stacie's sweet, soft voice echoed though his weak mind. His eyes slowly closed, but not because he was drifting off; it was because he had thought of something that he had not thought of before. He knew how lovely Stacie was, but there was something else he only now remembered—her perfume. Jason didn't know the name of that sweet smell, but his senses were able to recall its fragrance. That smell was heavenly—like roses near the open sea on a beautiful spring day, and he held onto it in his thoughts for as long as he could before he fell asleep.

Debbie let out a yawn, and Stacie told her that she should get to bed.

"No, it's okay. I can still talk if you want," Debbie said, "We never talk like this."

"No, you get some sleep. You have been like the big sister that you should be, and I thank you for that. Plus we did have to talk about mom before dad comes home. You have given me a lot to think about, and I do want Dad to come home to a loving family," she told Debbie.

"I know you do; we all do, and that's why you have to try to talk to her when you get a chance," Debbie said.

They said goodbye to each other and hung up. Debbie sat there for a moment and hoped that Stacie would stay true to her word, but Debbie knew that it would be hard for Stacie to ignore everything that she had told her. Debbie told herself that Stacie would do the right thing, and with that relaxation of her own thoughts, she sank back into the bedroom.

Jason was now fast asleep in the dark room that held very little light from the moon and dim streetlights; Debbie moved closer to her love and rested her head on his chest. She threw her left arm over him and fell asleep without any worries about Stacie.

After Stacie hung up the phone, she laid down on the leather sofa and flipped through the television channels looking for something good—something that would help her stay awake just a little longer so that she could think about what Debbie had told her while it was still fresh in her mind—but there was nothing on.

Stacie glanced over at the clock on the wall over the oak desk; the time read: eleven-fifty. She turned back to the television, and, still seeing nothing that caught her attention, closed her eyes. When she opened her eyes after a brief nap, a television show that she had not seen in years was playing.

That's an old show. I haven't seen the BEAV in years, she thought, sitting up and leaned forward.

Stacie sat there and watched it, and as she placed her hands on the sofa to change her position, the material under her palms felt like the old leather sofa her mom and dad had when she was growing up on the estate. It made her think of the time when she got a slap on the back of her hand for spilling her drink on it (apple juice was her favorite as a child). She remembered cleaning it up as the television show played on without her.

Stacie remembered how she had to go into the kitchen more than once to ring out the washcloth and then get the leather cleaner to finish cleaning the sofa like a maid. Stacie made sure that it was cleaned up right before she dared to call her mom into the room to give it a look-over. Margaret conducted the test of Stacie's cleaning as if she was conducting a bed inspection in a home for young girls. Stacie would have to stand by and watch her mother go over the Italian sofa with a fine-toothed comb. Stacie was also made to wipe down the kitchen table after she ate. She even cleaned up her room on weekends, but Debbie didn't have to do any of those things.

Stacie's mother only made her do this when her father was at work or out of town on business. When he was home, it was the maid who came in three times a week to clean Stacie's room. Margaret would still get Stacie to clean up after herself even when the maid had offered to do it, but this only happened when Richard was not around. There were times when she asked herself as a young girl why her mother would make her clean, but not Debbie. As time went on, she stopped asking herself that question because she thought her mother didn't like her. All Stacie wanted was her love, so she did whatever she was told in the hopes of winning it. Stacie just wanted to make her mother happy so that she would be loved just like Debbie.

"You make sure your room is nice and clean by the time I get back, Stacie," Margaret would tell her as she stood in front of the two large French doors of the estate. Stacie looked on and watched her young self waving goodbye to her mother as she left. It was then that she felt that thought was too vivid to be just a thought, because things in her mind were too clear. It was as if she was right there—as if she could reach out and touch them. Stacie was sure that image was something else, yet she didn't know what else it could be.

Do people think in their dreams as they stand within their dreams? Stacie asked herself. She received no answer, and she stood up and walked to her old bedroom. Her mother's room was at the end of the hallway; it never looked bright to her at the end of the hallway, even by the light of the lamp on the antique wooden table. Stacie looked down the long hallway for a moment before she decided to go to her mother's room. There were oil paintings of butterflies all down the hallway, and that was the one thing that Stacie loved looking at every single time she made her way down the hall. At the end of the hall, right near her mother's room was the nicest painting of them all; it had a misty background of white and light yellow, and dark branches that ran across the painting. Three butterflies of all different colors perched on the branches. Stacie reached up to touch the blue butterfly, and when she did, the color came off on her fingertips. She stepped back and pressed her fingertips together so she could feel the rich texture of the oil paint between them.

"I don't like this dream," she said as she turned the old copper doorknob with the paint still on her fingertips. Stacie pushed the door open and looked into her mother's room. Stacie just stood there looking into the dim room. Her childhood self ran past her, and the room brightened as she made her way into the room. Stacie looked on in awe as her younger self rummaged through her mother's things. Stacie had opened the door to her past, and was know watching it unfold before her eyes. Her memories flowed into the room like a flood, almost sweeping her away.

Stacie watched herself at the tender age of seven opening dresser drawers and trying on dresses that made her feel exquisite, and it was almost like watching an old film that didn't skip—not once. Even though the room was filled with sunlight, it was a dull light. That bright sun illuminated the entire room; it brought forward all the tiny particles of dust that slowly drifted through the air. Young Stacie danced around the room in the bright sunlight, and only stopped to look at herself in the tall, mirrored closet doors. She stepped back and examined herself; the mirror showed her a young, beautiful girl. As she stood in front of the sliding glass doors, she could almost hear something calling out to her.

Stacie gripped the doorframe as she watched little Stacie walk over to the far right side of the closet door and slide it open. Stacie felt the cold glass in her hand. That cold feeling soon turned into a warm sensation as her eyes found a glass jar inside a box, and there seemed to be something inside that jar that resembled animal hair. She placed one foot into the room, holding the doorframe a little tighter—a part of her just refused to let go. It was as if that doorframe wouldn't let her go. She began to feel that something wasn't right, and even though she could feel some fear in herself, she just couldn't understand how she could feel anything if this was all a dream.

Margaret had come back home and was making her way down the hallway. Stacie couldn't turn around to see who was coming from behind her, nor could she call out to her younger self in the closet. Margaret stormed past Stacie at the entrance of the room like a harsh wind blowing through the treetops in the dead of night. Stacie could see her mother standing in front of her with a look of rage on her face. It was still enough to drive the fear right into her heart. Stacie watched helplessly from the doorway as Margaret rushed up from behind her young daughter and pulled her out of the closet by her arm, throwing her to the floor. When Margaret pulled her out of the closet, young Stacie pulled the box along with her, and the glass jar shattered all over the floor. Margaret yelled at her to get out, and while little Stacie struggled to her feet, Margaret gave her a hard slap across the face.

At the doorway Stacie relived the pain and the memory that she had locked away for so long. All that yelling could be heard from the doorway, and she didn't need to hear it, because she had heard it so many times before.

Stacie watched her younger self run out of the room, wailing through strands of blond hair that were stuck to her face from her own broken-hearted tears; the pain in her face meant nothing. Stacie saw herself turn when she reached her bedroom door and looked back at her mother on her knees crying over the broken glass; it was something her young mind could not explain.

Ringing jolted Stacie out of her sleep. She opened her eyes and saw that the television screen was black and mirror-like in the dark room. It had been a dream all along.

No, Beav. It was just a dream, but it was so real. It felt so real, she thought as she dropped her pretty face into her trembling hands. She got up and squinted at the clock as her hands searched for the phone. It was ten after three in the morning, and by the time she found the phone half-under the loveseat, it had stopped ringing.

Could that have been Debbie, or a wrong number? Stacie didn't want to call and find out. It may not have been Debbie, and she didn't want to wake her. Stacie put the phone on the coffee table. She got her head together and walked to the washroom to get ready for bed. Stacie threw back the bed sheets and froze; her mind flashed back to her dream and she understood what she had seen as a child.

Hair, is that what was in that jar? Was it animal hair? Stacie thought as she gracefully slipped under the aqua blue satin sheets. *It was longer then fur. Like hair; human hair. Maybe it was a wig.*

Stacie didn't think too much about it as she fell back to sleep.

5

Debbie held her pill bottle up to her face as she stood in front of the bathroom mirror that held someone she didn't recognize. Her feet grew cold from standing on the traditional smoky-white marble floor. She had not taken a pill in two days, and she felt fine. Yet she knew that feeling would soon leave her—like that warm comfortable feeling leaving the body when you step out into the cold bitter winter air. If she didn't take one, her mood would change, and she could lose Jason. That would be too painful for her; it would feel like dying.

Jason was the best thing to happen to her in a long time, and she wanted it to last forever, like in a fairy tale. But her life was no fairy tale. She swallowed one of those pills and found that it tasted different somehow; it was bittersweet, and it made her want to regurgitate. She quickly took a drink of water and looked deeply into the mirror.

This has to stop, she thought, as she placed both hands on the sink. Debbie felt a little better after washing that pill down, but she didn't know how long it would last.

Jason was already in the kitchen. He had made breakfast and had the table already made. As Debbie walked into the kitchen, they looked at each other with love in their eyes, and passion still raging through their hearts. Debbie walked over to him and gave him a good morning kiss.

"Good morning, beautiful. Sit down and eat before it gets cold," Jason said as he pulled out her chair.

"I will, I just want to get a cup of coffee. It looks good, Jason. How long have you been up?" Debbie asked as she poured herself a cup of coffee.

"Not to long," Jason said turning to her and giving her a smile. He turned back around to his plate and continued to eat.

Debbie came back over to the table and sat down, keeping her gaze on Jason as she ate. He looked up at her and knew that she was going to ask him something; he had seen that look in her eyes before, it always meant the same thing.

"What is it? I hope… it's kinky," he said playfully.

"Jason, we're at the breakfast table, and no, it's not kinky. Not unless you've found a way to get all worked up over going to the hospital."

"The hospital? Why do you want me to go to the hospital?"

Debbie told him that she had to go to the doctor's and then to her mother's. She asked if he could pick up the little stuffed dog in the closet of her father's room. Jason said okay, but reminded her that he had to be at work on time. Debbie left before Jason, and then ten minutes later Jason got into his truck and headed to the hospital. On the way there Jason looked at the gas gauge and saw that it was very low.

"Shit," his eyes rolled back as the word left his mouth. "Now I have to find a fucking gas-station," Jason said with considerable frustration. He spotted an Esso on the corner. He pulled in and got gas as fast as he could before it got busy. He rushed inside to pay and that was when he saw the plants outside at the store next to the Esso station.

Jason quickly thought of Stacie as he paid for the gas, and as he walked back to the truck he looked over at them again. He got into his truck and drove next door to get a better look at the colorful plants that had caught his eye, and reminded him of Stacie. He stepped out of the truck and asked the lady inside what kind of plants they were that she had out front; he talked quickly, and the lady could tell that he was in a hurry.

"Iris plants," she told him.

Jason went out and picked one up as the lady's husband watched on. Jason didn't see him on his way in, but he was there now, and he looked at Jason like he was crazy, the way he was rushing around. He paid for the Iris and headed for the hospital.

On the way there he looked at the plant several times, and to him it looked just like the one Stacie had had in the room, except for one thing: the pot. That pot was a clay pot, and it was Chinese red. He couldn't take it back, and he was not going to. Jason would just have to tell Stacie about it the next time he saw her. He didn't want to upset her by telling her what he thought her mother had done.

I'll come up with something to tell her if it comes up, or when it comes up, he thought.

Jason went straight to the hospital and straight to the room; he got the little dog and left the plant right where the other one had been. It looked nice there, and it gave the room some life. Jason took a moment to look at Richard and think of what kind of a man he was. Jason said goodbye knowing that Richard couldn't hear him, and he left for work.

Jason didn't have to worry about Margaret seeing the plant, because if she had smuggled the plant out in her handbag—and Jason knew damn well that she had—then there would be no way for her to bring up the fact that it was a new plant, and try to find out who had brought it. Jason knew that if Stacie heard about it before she saw it that it would upset her; even seeing it would upset her, and that was when he knew that he would have to tell her no matter what. His intentions were good; they were just off, and it was because he had rushed around and not thought things through.

Jason was back home before three, and when he walked in the front door, he could hear Debbie talking on the phone.

"Jason?" Debbie called out, sounding surprised.

"Yes, it is I."

I thought you were going to stay at work all day," she asked.

"So did I, but I forgot all my French-curves here, so I told myself to come home and work," he told her and then he asked how the doctor's went.

"My doctor's appointment went okay, I guess. Same as before," she said.

"Sorry," he said as he held her. Jason worked late into the night and Debbie watched a movie; it was dark out and the trees loomed outside Jason's studio window. They moved in the warm breeze, and it gave him an idea for his project. Just as he started to draw out the idea, the phone rang. Debbie called out that she would get it. Jason worked on and didn't think of anything but his work, but he heard her talking in the background. He began to wonder who was on the other end of that phone. He stood up and walked over to the door; it sounded like she was talking to Stacie, but he wasn't sure. He returned back to his work and tried to get his head back into it, but couldn't.

Jason opened the window and looked into the dark, moonless night. That air felt a little cool even though it had been a warm day. He went out to the living room and flopped down on the sofa; Debbie was still on the phone, and she was looking right at him as she talked.

Debbie hung up and commented on how her family was too much. She said that it was bad enough that she had agreed to tell her sister when her own mother was going to the hospital, and now her mother was wanting to know if she was at the hospital today.

"Didn't you go and see her after seeing the doctor?" Jason asked.

"No, I just wanted to get home," she said sounding unhappy. "I told her that you were there, and she didn't say anything."

Jason didn't think that she would say anything; it was better that she had not. She only wanted to know who was there; she had said nothing about the plant, and he knew this to be true because Debbie would have said something.

They watched the movie and when it was over Debbie wanted to go to bed, and Jason returned back to his work. He worked until eleven-thirty, and then went into the kitchen to get a drink. He got a glass of milk and headed back through the living room. The phone began to ring. Jason was right by it, and picked it up on the first ring. He knew that if he had been in the studio, that it would have taken him some time to reach it, and Debbie would have woken up.

"Hello," he said in somewhat of a low voice.

"Hello, Jason. It's Stacie. How are you?"

"I'm doing good, Debbie is asleep," he told her.

"Oh, is she? I guess I can call back tomorrow. I just wanted to ask her something. Maybe you know?" Stacie asked him.

"Know what?"

Stacie then asked him if her mother had called there tonight, and Jason told her that she had. Jason couldn't hold it inside of him any longer. He feared that if he didn't say something that it would come back and haunt him, and make Debbie angry with him for going against her instructions. Jason told Stacie that he had to explain something to her, but not right now while Debbie was nearby.

"Is it something to do with Debbie?" Stacie asked with great concern in her voice.

"No, no, Debbie is fine. It's something that I have done that I shouldn't have done. I will explain everything if you have the time to talk," he told her.

Stacie agreed and gave Jason her cell number. She told him that she was off for two days, and that he could call her at any time. They said goodbye and Jason went back to work. He finished up in the studio and went to bed, and as he pulled the covers up over him, he couldn't even look over at Debbie with Stacie so clear in his mind.

By lunchtime the next day, Jason had finished showing the designs to a new client, and when they left Jason went to a small office to call Stacie. It didn't take her long to pick up the phone; it was as if she was waiting beside it for him to call. As if she were waiting to hear his voice again, the voice she had thought about more then once--the one she was attracted to. Jason felt uneasy about this, but he had to try to set the situation right.

"Hello, Jason," Stacie said as she held the phone close to her ear and her antique-ruby-red lips.

"Hello, Stacie. I hope this is a good time for you," Jason asked.

"Yes," she said, anxious to hear what he had to say.

Jason explained that he had seen Margaret smuggling the Iris plant out of the hospital in her handbag, and how it had made him feel. Jason then told her that he knew that she would feel hurt, so he bought another Iris plant and put it in the room, to beat Margaret at her own game. She fell silent for a moment, but then spoke, "I knew she would do something like that. It's just like the pillow I took for him. It will be the same if I take something else as well."

Jason didn't know about the pillow, or what had transpired between Margaret and Stacie over it, and he was not going to be foolish enough to ask; he already put his nose too far into this family already.

"I'm sorry if I was out of line by buying the plant," Jason said breaking the silence.

"Jason, there is no need to say sorry. What you did was very sweet, and I thank you for caring for how I feel. Debbie's lucky to have someone like you in her life," Stacie said.

"Thanks." He did not know what else to say, but Stacie did.

"I sometimes think about the other day when we were on the elevator, and that old man. It's funny now in my head, more-so than it was on the day it happened," she told him.

"Really?"

"Yes, sometimes it just comes to me. Like the other day in the middle of a photo shoot."

"Told you that it was somewhat funny," Jason, replied.

They talked a little longer and she seemed happy and comfortable with him; her shyness was now gone, and in a way, it was never really there with Jason to begin with. Before they said their goodbyes, she asked if Debbie was home, because she needed to ask her something. Jason told her that she should be, but he was not sure if she had anything to do today. Stacie said that she would try the house phone, and for him not to worry--she wouldn't let her know that they had talked.

"I liked talking to you, Jason. I would have asked someone about the plant, and still not have been upset."

"I enjoyed talking to you as well," Jason replied.

"I feel that I should do something for you, for being so sweet and caring about my feelings. How about a coffee on me one day?"

Jason didn't know what to say, but his heart did, and it spoke through him. "That would be nice, but I don't know," he said.

"It's just coffee, Jason. It's okay. You were so nice enough to buy a new plant for me, so let me buy you coffee."

"Okay, I guess you're right."

"Okay, so I'll let you know when. Goodbye for now, Jason. Talk to you soon," she said.

"Goodbye, Stacie."

Stacie called Debbie and was a little unsure of how she was going to ask her what she needed to know, but she knew she needed to ask her somehow.

Debbie picked up and said hello in a voice that was her own, but when she heard Stacie on the other end, her tone changed.

"How are you, Stacie?"

"I'm fine, are you okay?" Stacie asked, but didn't get an answer.

"So, just to let you know, mom won't be at the hospital for the next two days."

"Thank you, Debbie, but that's not what I was calling about."

"Oh, so what are you calling about?" Debbie asked."

Stacie didn't know how to say it, so she just said it. She asked Debbie if Mom ever wore a wig. Debbie laughed and told her that she was funny, but Stacie was serious and Debbie could soon tell. Debbie then thought about it, but could not come up with anything, and then she asked Stacie why she was asking her these things.

"Because I had a dream the other night and I remembered something that I had forgotten," she told her.

Debbie didn't know what to say at first, but then said, "You were the one that was always in her room getting all dolled-up, you should know," Debbie said in a voice that didn't sound like hers.

"I know that I was, but there was a glass jar and it looked like fur or hair in it. I think it was hair, because it was straight," she explained.

Debbie asked if this was in the dream or when she was young. Stacie said it was in her dream, but it was a dream of what had happened when she was young. Debbie told her that as far as she could remember mom never wore a wig, and that it was just a dream. Debbie asked if she was even trying to work things out with their mother, and Stacie said that she would, but that she had not as of yet.

"Stacie, you said you would."

"I know I did, but this has nothing to do with that," Stacie said, not fully understanding why Debbie wasn't even trying to hear her out.

"Stacie, I'm not trying to call you a liar, I just can't remember anything like that in her room. I wasn't even allowed in there, not at all, even when dad was home," Debbie told her.

"Dad never let you in their bedroom?" Stacie asked. She tried to think if he ever let her in the room, but just could not remember that part of her childhood.

"Stacie, just work on you and Mom getting along. That's all you should be thinking about," Debbie told her.

Stacie did not say anything and could only think about why Debbie was not listening to her. Stacie had seen it in a dream, yes, but it was something that had actually happened.

Stacie said goodbye in dismay. How could Debbie just blow her off, even if Debbie did not see it that way? Stacie should have just kept on talking to Jason; at least he made her feel wanted.

Maybe I'll try and talk to her later. I can't see why she wouldn't listen to what I have to say. Yet, in a way I can see it, because she has always been the favorite, Stacie thought as she grabbed her light spring coat and left her lavish condo apartment for a day of shopping and a visit to her father.

Stacie returned home just after eight. Even though it was late, it was still light out when she pulled into the underground parking. She made it onto the elevator and up to her apartment with all her bags. Stacie just dropped the bags in the entranceway and made a dash for the washroom. When she came out she walked past her fancy retro home phone and stopped.

Maybe I should call her. Should I call her? I should try. Debbie wants me to try, Stacie thought as her hand touched the phone. Stacie picked up the phone and called her mom; it seemed like it was ringing and ringing forever, yet it only rang two times.

"Hello," Margaret said as she picked up the phone.

"Hello, Mom."

"Stacie?"

"Yes, it's me. How are you?"

"What would you like, Stacie? I'm busy and can't talk for long," Margaret said in a cold voice.

"Okay, well . . . I'll let you go then, and I love you, Mom."

"Goodbye, Stacie, and goodnight," Margaret said, and then hung up.

Stacie stood there holding the phone for a moment and then hung it up.

"There, Debbie, I called her . . . just like you wanted."

6

Debbie woke in the middle of the night and turned to Jason; she couldn't help but think of things that had happened to her in her life, things that depressed her. Her father being in a coma, and a sister unable to reconcile with their mother, and a feeling of sickness that sat in the depths of her belly from those pills she took.

She did nothing but lie there as she yearned for alcohol that she had not had in a long time, and it had been a long time because she had been on Aripiprazole for over a year now. Debbie was slowly getting off those pills against her doctor's orders. She was feeling fine, but they always upset her stomach when she took them. This was not always the case, however. At first they didn't make her feel this way, but as the year passed by and her mood disorder became less and less potent, the feeling of physical sickness became stronger and stronger. Feeling physically sick became a daily occurrence. Debbie feared falling into drinking if she stopped taking her pills, but that thought wasn't always with her. The craving for a drink took hold of her in those moments when she lost her vigilance.

Debbie had been through this when she lived on her own in the house that Margaret bought for her. It was in that house and at that time that she tried to take her own life. It happened one day in May after she'd drunk away her sadness in the living room. She had passed out and woken up hours later with thoughts of suicide dancing in her head. She felt that her life was hopeless. Debbie had just lost her boy-friend of five years, and she couldn't shake the idea that her life had no promise. Living alone just made things worse.

If it were not for Margaret, Debbie would have died in that house. Margaret had a key to the house and went over one day to see if she was okay after failing to get a hold of her on the phone. Margaret found Debbie on the living room floor with liquor on the coffee table and a syringe by her side.

Debbie was rushed to the hospital were she stayed for some time under close watch, because the doctors felt she was trying to kill herself. After she was released from the hospital, she went to a psychiatrist with Margaret. The doctor had her put on Aripiprazole right away, but it took time for the pills to work. It was in that time that Debbie showed herself capable of not only hurting herself, but also other people. A man in the grocery store was in a hurry to pay for his things and leave, and had pushed into line and insulted her, telling her to go to hell when she protested. Debbie lost her temper and struck him in the face with her fist, but that was the only time that happened.

Debbie came out of her thoughts and got out of bed. She went downstairs and looked around for what her body was craving. All she could find was a bottle of red wine that Jason's uncle made over a year ago. She took a drink; it was very strong, but that was okay with her because her craving was equally strong. Debbie only had one glass and then put the bottle back where she'd found it.

Debbie found herself wandering aimlessly around the dark silent house thinking about what she had just done, and about how Jason knew nothing of her alcoholic past—a past mixed with drugs. She thought that if Jason knew about her past that he would leave her. Debbie told herself that she would not fall into that dark place again, and that she would take her pills as often as she could without feeling sick. She felt that if she did that, then she would be able to control it; she would be its master, not its servant.

Debbie felt bad about how she had talked to Stacie. She regretted not hearing her out, Debbie realized that she couldn't see how she was acting. Debbie believed that that one drink helped her see her thoughts more clearly. She put the glass in the dishwasher and made sure that everything in the kitchen was the way it was before she set foot in it. Debbie made her way back to bed, but she just lied there thinking of things. She couldn't sleep. She didn't think that those pills pushed her to the point of drinking. It wasn't because she enjoyed drinking, or that it put her at ease; she saw it as her family pushing her to the point that she needed to drink in order to cope. She wished that there were a way to escape from her life and start over again with Jason by her side. She loved her mother and sister, but couldn't solve the conflict between them. Debbie lay there and almost forgot that her love was beside her. The truth was that she couldn't bear to look at him after sneaking around the house looking for a drink; it was then that she knew she had to get a handle on her drinking.

Two days had passed and Debbie had only taken one pill, yet she felt fine. Debbie was about to run to the store when the phone rang. She closed the door and answered it.

"Hello."

"Hello, Debbie. It's Mother."

"Hi, how are you?" Debbie asked.

Margaret told her that she was fine and well, and so was father, despite still being in a coma. Debbie told her that it would be fine, and that before she knew it he would be back home.

"Stacie will love that," Margaret commented.

"Well, yes, she will…we all will," Debbie told her.

Margaret told Debbie that was exactly the point. Stacie would love it, and Richard would love to see all of them, but he would especially love to hold his little girl longer than anyone else.

Debbie listened to her mother ramble on about Stacie, and on the outside she didn't want to hear it, but on the inside she knew that Margaret was right. Growing up, Stacie had occupied all of her father's attention, and been given everything that she wanted. That was one of the facts of Debbie's life.

Margaret then asked Debbie if she had heard from her sister in the last couple of days. Debbie told her that she had not. Margaret went on to tell her that Stacie had called her the other day, and that Margaret had told her that she couldn't talk.

"Why would you do that? Maybe she wants to work things out between you two? You two never talk, and it's hard on us all, even father."

"You shouldn't worry about your father. He knows the way things are in this family, and has always known. It is not hard on him," Margaret told Debbie.

Debbie heard her, but didn't quite understand.

"Are you saying that he knows why you and Stacie are not getting along?"

"No, nothing like that. I know we should get along, but your sister really knows how to get under my skin. She has always been like this, but not you, Debbie. You're my little angel."

"I know I am, Mother, but you have to try and talk to her sometime," Debbie said, hoping that she would in time.

"I know, and I will, but not now. I have too many things on my mind…you know that, right?"

Debbie did know that and didn't push the issue any further. Margaret asked how her and Jason were doing, and if he was busy at work. Debbie told her that they were just fine, and that Jason must be busy, because he had been leaving an hour before her every morning for the past two days.

* * *

Jason sat in his pick-up truck and waited for Stacie's Jaguar to pull into the parking lot. He didn't think of the time that had gone by, and he didn't really care. It was only coffee and talking, but they both knew that behind the morning drinks and all that talking lurked forbidden passion just waiting to be set free.

Stacie arrived on time, as always, and parked across from Jason. She stepped out of that carnelian Jag and walked over to his truck. Jason got out and said hello. They then went inside for their coffee.

They sat down at a far table after getting their coffee and looked at each other for a long time without saying a word. They were attracted to each other, and they could no longer hide it.

"Were you late for work the other day?" she asked.

"No, I was right on time," he replied.

"Sorry about the long drive, but this place makes the best cappuccino."

Jason agreed, this place made good coffee. Coffee that was to die for, but he also knew that she did not want to chance anyone that they knew seeing them together. Jason was okay with that, because he did not want Debbie to know he was having coffee with her sister.

They talked about things that had nothing to do with the family. They talked about places in the world that they have traveled, and Stacie had been to more places than Jason.

"That's not fair. You're a beautiful model. It's, like, your job to go to different places."

"No it's not. I do most of my work right here, near home," she told him, and then she asked, "Jason are you a movie buff?"

"Yes, I love movies, and I watch them all the time. More then once a week if it's a real good one," he told her.

"I love movies too, but I hate watching them alone," she looked into his eyes, hoping that he would be able to read them. She hoped he would ask her. Stacie knew that it was wrong to want that, but he was everything she was looking for in a man.

Jason told her that he would love to see one with her, but that it would not be right. Coffee was one thing, but a movie was like a date.

"Maybe we can put a rain check on the movie for now, if you want," she suggested.

Jason asked if he could call her to let her know when he wanted to go, and she said yes. They finished their coffees and headed out to the parking lot.

"Well, thank you for the coffee, Stacie," he said as she looked downwards. "Are you okay?" Jason then asked.

"Yes, I…just love my sister, and I—" Stacie could not push the words out, and found it hard. "I…well, you know," she then said, looking up at him.

"I'm starting to."

"You are?" Stacie asked looking into his eyes.

"Yes, but I have the same problem as you do."

"What is that? Stacie asked.

"I love Debbie as well. Yet I'm falling for someone else," he told her.

"I see. Could you see yourself with this person?" Stacie asked as she moved a little closer to him.

"Yes, but I can't for the life of me understand how this person I'm falling for is not already with someone else, because she is so beautiful."

Maybe she has been alone for a long time, and is looking for someone special––someone that will treat her right. Maybe she feels that special person is you," Stacie said. Jason moved towards her, and as he did, Stacie leaned into him, and they kissed for the first time. It was not a long kiss, but it felt like time stopped for them.

Jason could not help himself, this was what his heart had been longing for, and as he kissed her, the feeling of wanting her for so long left his body. He could not believe how soft and smooth her light coral pink lips were. As they pulled away from each other, he could see that Stacie was now looking up at him.

"So…I'll give you a call," Jason said, looking into her eyes.

"Okay, and maybe we can talk about a movie if you don't feel like actually seeing one," she said to him with a smile.

Jason smiled back and said goodbye. She also said goodbye, and as Jason walked over to his truck on legs that felt like rubber, his heart was now hers for the taking.

That night, Jason dreamed only of Stacie and how he had kissed her. As he dreamed, Debbie was downstairs getting a drink. It made her feel free, and all she had to do was keep it from her mother and Jason.

Jason woke to find himself alone in bed; he got up and looked around the room. He could see that her slippers were gone, and wondered to himself where she had gone. He assumed that she would have to be downstairs. He couldn't smell anything, so she was not cooking, so he got up and headed downstairs.

"Debbie," he called out as he reaches the bottom of the stairs, but nobody answered him.

Those blizzard blue drapes were still closed, which was a little odd to him, because Debbie always opened them as soon as she came downstairs to let the new day come in.

Jason opened them and when he turned around, he saw Debbie passed out on the sofa.

"Debbie," he called out to her. She opened her eyes, and then sat up.

"You slept down here last night?" he asked as she just sat there taking a deep breath.

She did not say anything. She stood up and walked into the kitchen; Jason followed. He asked her if she would like a cup of tea or coffee, and she said no. This was new to Jason, and he wondered to himself if she knew about the kiss that he and Stacie had shared at the coffee shop miles away.

Debbie swung open the stainless steel fridge door and just stood looking inside. Jason asked if it was the pills; he knew that they made her stomach upset and that the doctor would not change them because he told her that it would pass. She took out the milk and sat down at the table, but she did not get a cup.

"Debbie what is it? What is wrong?"

"I just don't feel well," she told him in a low voice.

"Well then you should go lie down and just rest," Jason told her.

"I have things to do today. I can't just lay around," she said.

Jason told her that he would do them for her, and that he would go out and get that chicken noodle soup that she liked. She said okay, but what Jason did not know was that it would take more than soup to cure Debbie's ills.

Debbie went up to bed, but not before she gave Jason a kiss and telling him that she loved him. He watched her walk up the stairs, and she looked back at him on her way up. Jason could not help but think of Stacie, and Margaret. Margaret's voice could be heard in Jason's head and he did not like it.

She's pretty. Do you think she is pretty?

He could hear her voice right in the middle of his mind; it was hard to push it out. It was like having water in his ear. He hoped it would go away with time.

The house phone rang and Jason picked it up quickly. The voice on the other end helped Jason forget about what Margret had said to him in the past.

"Hello, Stacie," Jason said.

"Hello, how are you?" Stacie asked. She had called to talk to Debbie, but was pleased to hear Jason's voice instead.

He whispered that he missed her, and she told him the same. Stacie asked if Debbie was around, and Jason told her that she was not feeling well. He told Stacie that he noticed that Debbie seemed different somehow. Stacie asked him if it was the flu, and he told her that it was, and that he was just on his way out to get her some soup.

"Do you know if she has been drinking?" Stacie asked.

"Drinking? What are you talking about?" Jason asked with great surprise.

"She has never told you about her drinking?"

"No. I thought the pills were for her depression?"

Stacie told him that if Debbie was home, that he should not talk about it. He asked if they could get together later in the day to discuss it, because he wanted to know what was going on with her. Stacie told

Jason that when he was ready, he could come over to her place and they would talk about it. Jason was more than happy, and agreed.

"Do you have a pen to write down my address?" Stacie asked.

"Yes," Jason said as he held the ballpoint pen with shaky fingers.

"I'm at 275 Rockwell Towers, apartment 7A. Buzzer number is also 7A. Do you know where that is?"

"Yes, I have been down there once or twice," he told her.

"So . . . I'll see you soon?" Stacie asked in a low voice.

"Yes I'll be there shortly."

Jason hung up the phone and went up to the bedroom to make sure Debbie was okay. He really went up to make sure that she had not overheard him, and he was reassured to see that she was fast asleep. Jason returned downstairs and went out to the truck. He puts the key in the door and just stood there for a moment.

Is this really happening? How can this be happening? I wanted to have her, and now I'm going to her place to talk to her, he thought as he slowly turned the key to unlock the truck door.

He went straight to the address that Stacie had given him and parked in the visitor's lot; the building was tall, too tall, he thought, for a condominium. Jason often worked around condos, and they were never this tall, or this nice. Jason followed the fancy stone walkway to the front lobby doors, and could not get over the two small ponds on either side of the walkway. They had fish in them, not a lot, but enough to bring the two ponds to life.

Jason walked in through the doors and into the lobby. He checked the paper he had written her address on, and he reached his shaky pointer finger out to push the numbers.

"Hello," a voice said through the intercom. It was Stacie, but it didn't sound like her.

"Hello, Stacie. It's Jason."

"Hello. Seventh-floor," she said, and buzzed him in.

Jason opened the large glass door that reminded him of the shower doors back at the house, but on the other side of these glass doors was a man behind a counter. He called Jason over and asked him for the floor number and the last name of the person on that floor. Jason could see that there was another glass door that he had to pass through before he could get onto the elevator... and to Stacie.

"Floor seven," he told the man.

"Okay, and the last name,"

"Whiting," Jason said as he looked around at the lobby that was in the shape of a large *L*.

"Okay, sir, you can head on up," the young man said as he looked up from his computer.

"Thank you," Jason said and then walked towards the glass doors. As he approached the doors, they buzzed. Jason pulled one open and walked through. He got onto the elevator, and went up to Stacie's floor. He thought about the door number in his mind. He imagined doors up and down the hallway with question marks on them where the numbers should have been.

Jason could tell that the apartments were large just from standing in the long, wide, and well-lit hallway. He saw Stacie at her door and walked over to her.

"Hi," Jason said, looking at her. He could not move for a moment; he could not believe that he was at her place, and could not believe that he was once again near her. She looked different somehow; her eye shadow was new, and he could tell that her lips were a little darker, but she still looked breathtaking.

"Did you have a hard time getting in?" Stacie asked as they went inside.

"No. It just took some time, that's all."

"Sorry about that. Security is a big thing around here," she told him, "make yourself at home, Jason."

Jason looked around at her apartment and did not know what to say; it was big and very luxurious.

"Would you like a drink?" Stacie asked.

"Just ice water please, that would be great," Jason said as he walked through the apartment.

Stacie came back and handed him his ice water. In her hand she was holding a glass with a kiwi wedge on it.

"What is that?" He asked.

"A little health drink I make," she said. "Let me show you around, and then I'll fix you one. You will love it."

Stacie showed Jason around and he could still not believe that this was an apartment. They went back into the living room and sat down on the leather sofa, and that was when Jason asked what it was that she wanted to tell him about Debbie.

Stacie started off by telling Jason that Debbie had gone through a lot in the past with drinking, and that she had been sober for about a year and a half. If she was drinking again, that meant that she was not taking her pills. Stacie told him that Debbie had gone through this before. Stacie told him that it was their mother that had seen it coming, and had stopped it. Debbie just had to take her pills.

Jason told Stacie that Debbie was always complaining that her pills made her feel sick, and that her doctor would not change them because she needed to be on those specific ones.

"I never knew that," Stacie said with a defeated look on her face. "It's so hard with her when she gets like this, and we don't even know what it is that's pushing her to be so unhappy."

Jason didn't understand it himself, but he knew one thing for sure: he knew that if Debbie ever found out about him getting close to her sister, that it would be the one thing that would drive her over the edge.

Stacie told him about the time Margaret found Debbie passed out in her old house from drinking and doing drugs, and that it happened before she was on any medication.

Jason had to take a minute to think if there was any liquor in the house, and as he sat there it came to him: *the wine.*

"If it gets to the point where you can't handle it Jason, you should call Margaret. She'll take care of Debbie just like she did before. Maybe just talk to her sometime when you get a chance, and let her know what you think is going on with, Debbie" Stacie said as she put her glass on the coffee table and asked if he was okay. Jason's eyes showed her that he was okay. He held his beaming gaze on her, and as he sat there beside her unable to move, she slowly reached out and took his hand into hers.

"I'll take care of it when I get home. I'll have to dump the wine bottles, if that's what she has been drinking," Jason told Stacie. Stacie ran her fingers up and down the top of his hand.

"Jason," she started to say, "how did you feel after you left the coffee shop the other day?"

"Good, I couldn't forget about the kiss, and it stayed with me for the rest of the day. You have been in my mind all this time," he told her.

Stacie told Jason that she had been thinking of him as well. She leaned forward to kiss him, and as she did, Jason quickly embraced her and pulled her into his body. Stacie kissed him savagely as she bit at his neck. She broke free from him and stood up, taking his hand so that he also stood up. She held on tight to Jason's hand, and led him to here room where Jason slowly undressed her.

Jason's hands glided over her smooth, firm body, as she lay naked on her bed. He kissed her softly, all over, from head to toe, and back up to her soft lips.

Stacie kissed him softly and bit at Jason's chest as he moved on top of her. Right at that moment he fell into that world that he had been in before, but this time it was with the person that was in his thoughts.

Jason made love to her longer then he had made love to Debbie, and as he embraced Stacie in his arms, he held no thought of Debbie in his mind and no memory of the love they had shared only days ago.

7

Jason drove back home with a hot bowl of soup in the passenger's seat, and no remorse in his heart. The warmth from Stacie's love ran through him like hot soup, and it's healing powers would stay with him for days.

As Jason pulled into the driveway, he could only hope that Debbie was still asleep, because be did not want to see her. Jason wanted some time to himself, but he had to bring her the soup, so he put on a good face and went up to her.

Jason made his way into the dimly-lit house, and knew right away that Debbie was still in bed. He closed his eyes, then slowly opened them and looked at the stairs. He looked down at the soup, then up the staircase again.

"Debbie, I'm back. I have your soup. Are you up?" he called out to her as he began to climb the flight of stairs.

She was still fast asleep after all this time, so he left the soup on the end table and went to go take a shower. He had to wash away the fragrance of Stacie, something that he had not thought of until now.

Margaret was at the beach house watching the waves come into the shoreline. They always made her think of the past, and of her sister. Margaret could almost see the two of them walking side by side down the beach with two little girls following close behind, but there had been times when it was just the two of them.

Margaret could remember the conversations and the way that they would laugh at one another's silly humor.

A long time ago, she thought as she got up and walked down the stretch of beach with a margarita in her hand.

Her sister was not the only person on her mind; there was one person that stood out more within her thoughts. Stacie was in there—it was a thought she did not want, but it was also a thought she could not remove. Margaret began to wonder what it was that Stacie had wanted the other day when she had called. Margaret was not going to phone her and find out, so all she could do was ponder it herself, or try to find out through Debbie.

Margaret walked on that warm sand looking over at the boat dock and she could not hold back her laughter; it was the dock that made her remember something that had been gone for so long from within her mind.

"What family has a dock and a small boat house, but no boat?"

"Maybe a family that ran out of money, or wood," Margaret and her sister would say to one another, and laugh over it all the way back to the beach house.

It was those sweet moments that kept her coming back to the beach, and to that feeling of being close to her sister. Margaret only felt her sister's nearness when she walked on the beach, and those sweet memories were there as well.

She did not walk for long today, and she moved faster than most days. Once she reached the end, Margaret went right back to the house. Something was gnawing at her; something that had not came to her before. Margaret did not like it. She did not want these thoughts in her mind while she walked the beach with the good thoughts of her sister still in her mind. There were times when she would come to the beach and hold only bad memories of the past deep down inside herself.

Margaret could not come up with what Stacie could have wanted, so she headed back to the beach house to find out. As soon as she got inside, she called Debbie, but Jason picked up as soon as it rang.

"Hello," Jason said.

"Hello, Jason. It's Mrs. Whiting. May I speak to Debbie?" she asked.

Jason had just come downstairs. Though he thought he'd heard Debbie waking up, he was unsure; he was sure of one thing, though. He knew that if she had been drinking, the soup would not help her right now. He told Margaret that he would go and see if she was awake, because she was not feeling well. Jason went back upstairs and could hear her in the shower.

"She is in the shower. Can I have her call you back when she gets out?"

"Yes, just tell her that I need to speak to her about something," Margaret said, and then hung up without saying goodbye.

Jason hung the phone up and started to wonder if Margaret knew anything about him and Stacie. Deep down he knew that would be impossible, and that it was just his mind and heart starting to feel guilty for what he had done. Still, he knew that if he had the chance to do it over again…he would.

He waited for Debbie to come downstairs before telling her that her mother had called. He also told her that her soup was on the end table. She hugged him and thanked him, but did not ask him what her mother had wanted. Jason made a cup of coffee and asked how she was feeling. Debbie told him that she was feeling much better, and that the soup would help. He stood there studying her and could see now that she had been drinking, but could not say anything because she would wonder how he knew about her past.

After she ate her soup, she called her mother. Jason was in the other room, but he could hear everything, and he was relieved to hear that it had nothing to do with him. They were talking about Stacie, and how Debbie had told Stacie to call and to try to talk to Margaret.

From what Jason could gather, Margaret was not happy. It seemed that Margaret had a feeling that Debbie had told Stacie to call her, because Stacie never called her unless Margaret had called her first. It should not have been that way, but it was, what it was, and it was not going to change anytime soon.

They did not discuss it for long, and then Debbie walked into the living room and sat down next to Jason. She did not say anything, but soon had to because Jason moved over a little and asked if she was okay.

"Yes, I had told Stacie to call Mother and try to work things out between the two of them, and Mother didn't like that very much. She asked that I never do that again," she explained to Jason.

Margaret sat and pondered what Debbie had done. Even though her intentions were noble, they were not good enough for Margaret. In Margaret's mind, she could not let go of the anger and hate that she held inside for Stacie. It was all because she felt Stacie knew too much about the family's past.

There were times when Stacie would walk in on Margaret when she was changing, and Margaret would yell at her to get out. Margaret never let the girls see her like that; she never wanted them to see the scars that ran down her back. Margaret had those scars from when she was young; it was from the fence on her grandfather's farm.

Margaret began to remember that day when she and her sister stayed at the farm for a week. Their grandfather made them work very hard. Margaret was always defiant about helping out. She never helped out at home, so she never wanted to help out on the farm. Margaret thought at a young age that maids did all the work, that was how it was in her world. But in her grandfather's home, maids and large rooms did not exist, nor did high-end cars.

He had yelled at her one time and chased her across the field for not doing as she was told. When she arrived at a fence, she tried to squeeze her way through the barbed wire and got stuck. Her grandfather did not know at the time that she was stuck—so he told her mother and father—and pulled her back through the fence, tearing her back open on the barbed wire. He quickly rushed her back to the farmhouse and got his wife to tend to her. And even though it happened years ago, she can still see the look on her grandfather's old face, the look of fear.

She never saw her grandfather after that, and her sister never saw him either. Margaret could remember looking at him for what would be the last time as her father drove away from the farmhouse and left her grandparents standing side-by-side, watching the car drive off down the dirt road. Not once did the girls look out the back window at them. The girls could see their grandparents' legs, however, in the rearview mirror.

There was talk through the family that the girls' grandfather had hit them from time to time. When Margaret and her sister were asked about it, it was Margaret who spoke for the both of them, and told her mother and father that he had hit them. Peg had told them that he warned them to never tell anyone about it. It was not long after that that the family turned their back on him for treating the girls like work tools, and injuring Margaret's back—all because she did not want to do what she did not have to do.

Margaret came out of her little daze. That thought helped her think about how hard she was on Stacie. Still, she did not want her to know about her past, and the other things that had come from it; the barbed wire fence was an accident, and was nothing to hide, but everything that came from that accident had to be hidden from young eyes and ears.

Margaret had always liked Debbie more, and Stacie would have to understand that one day. Liking Debbie more had nothing to do with being the oldest; it was just something that had always been a part of Margaret's way of thinking. It was not going to change just because Debbie wanted it to, especially not with a phone call. If Margaret could, she would show Debbie why she wanted Stacie out of her life. But that was not an option, and she had nothing on Stacie to use against her. Margaret would never be able to get dirt on Stacie to show Debbie, and she knew that saying something against someone to get what you wanted—like what was said against her grandfather—was the best way to remove someone from your family, or your life. For Margaret, achieving Stacie's downfall would be a pleasure. It was something that she had wanted for a long time.

8

Two days had passed since Jason started keeping an eye on the wine bottles, and he noticed that one of those wine bottles was getting low. He took the bottle and poured the entire thing down the drain in the kitchen sink. He then took the rest of the bottles and did the same. He had a feeling that there was one more bottle somewhere in the house, but he did not have a clue where Debbie would have put it.

Jason put the empties on the table one at a time, but had to stop to answer the phone. The timing was just right, he had just emptied the last bottle before it rang. Jason put the phone up to his ear and he heard Debbie's voice on the other end. Debbie asked him if he was going to stay home for the day, or if he had to return to work, because she needed to talk to him. He told her that he would remain at home until she got back; however, after they talked he would have to go to work.

Debbie was not far from the house, and before Jason knew it, she was walking through the front door. Debbie walked right up to him and hugged him as if she had not seen him in days. Through her eyes and deep within her mind that may have been true.

"I'm slipping, Jason. I'm trying, really I'm trying," Debbie blurted out. "I ... I thought I could handle it, but it's just like before."

"Debbie, calm down," Jason told her as he held her. "Where were you before you came home? Are you okay?"

Debbie told Jason that she went to the park so that she would not be in the house, because she knew that she would drink if she were home. She told him that she had a history of drinking, and had been doing fine up until a week ago. Debbie explained that she had not been taking her pills regularly, and that she thought this was causing her breakdown. Debbie was falling apart in Jason's arms and needed him now more than ever before.

Jason could not understand how all of this could happen to someone in just a short time, but then it came to him. She must have been off her pills longer than what she was actually telling him.

"You have to start taking your pills, Debbie," he said to her as she pulled her brown hair away from her tear-stained face. Her hair looked matted, and he could tell that she had not had a shower yet.

"You don't have to worry about the wine, okay. I've already got rid of it, all of it," he told her. "I had a feeling that something was going on with you, and after seeing how my brother went downhill from drinking, I knew right away that you must be drinking as well."

"I'm sorry, Jason. It was just there, and I..."

"Okay, it's over, but you should go back to the doctor's and see if he can put you on a different type of pill," Jason told her.

Debbie told him what the doctor had told her, and how he explained to her that it takes time for pills to start working within your system.

Jason told her to start taking them, and that they would get through this. She asked in fear if he was going to leave her, and he told her that if she did not get this under control, that he would have to. He knew he should not have told her that, but he did, that was just how it came out.

"I'm sorry for saying that, but I lost my brother to drinking, and I know what it can do to a person," he told her.

Debbie sat on the sofa and cried into her cold, clammy hands. It was hard to see her like this, and Jason could not stand by and watch her destroy herself. He went over to her, hoping that he could comfort her in some way. He also wanted to comprehend what she was going through, but he could not see past the drinking. The fact that she was drinking obscured her depression in his eyes. She began to say things with her face still in her hands, and Jason tried to put the words together.

"What is it? Debbie, I can't understand what you're trying to say when your head is down," he told her as she tried to lift her sad and weary head.

Debbie reflected on the past and then opened her world to Jason. She started to tell him of her life as a young child in the Whiting family. She was so young, and so unhappy, and always wanted her father's love, but found that it was hard to get. Stacie was by far Daddy's little girl—his princess with the long, flowing, beautiful blond hair—and Debbie always felt like one of the ugly stepsisters from that classic Walt Disney film.

"I know I shouldn't hold these thoughts inside, but he just seemed to be there for her more then he was for me when I was young," she explained.

Debbie lifted her head again and told Jason how she would sit in front of her bedroom mirror and wish that she were someone else, because then maybe her father would miss her. Debbie remembered that her mother was always there for her, and almost took on the role of a father for her.

It was not hard to see who Richard loved the most, yet it puzzled her at that young age. As the girls got older, Richard changed and started to see both girls as the same. He spent what time he could with both of them, and took them to the movies and shopping at Toys 'R' Us whenever he had free time away from work. The best times were when they would just go out for pizza and then buy a movie and watch it at home with a big bowl of popcorn and drinks.

"I can still recall those days," Debbie said.

"Those are very nice memories," Jason said to her as he thought of his own childhood.

Debbie went on, telling him that it was nice, and even though it was the perfect father-daughter day, Stacie was still their father's best little girl.

"Father would always ask her things first, no matter what it was. 'What movie would you like to see, Stacie? Debbie…is there one that you would like to see? Stacie, pick any toy you want sweetheart. You too, Debbie. Pick something nice,' it was like that all the time," she told Jason.

"I don't think he meant it like you were second best, Debbie. You got to know that he loves you right?" Jason asked her. He watched her going over it in her mind as if she was doing a long calculation of the past, and her face showed it.

"I know he loves me," she finally said, "but it's just how I feel about it all, and what I saw growing up."

"Your mother loves you more then anything, even more than Stacie. I'm not saying it's right, but you have always had her love."

"Yes, I have always had her to talk to, but I never told her how I felt. And yes, I have seen how hard she was—and is—on Stacie, regardless of what was going on in the house. There was a time when she wasn't there for me, however—a time when I really needed her," Debbie said.

Debbie began to tell Jason of the time when she was around ten, and the family spent the weekend up at the beach house; it was a weekend that showed her that something undoubtedly was wrong with her emotions. Debbie told him how she woke up early and went outside to be alone; being in the large bedroom was not alone enough for her. She walked down to the beach, and then she walked to the boat dock and sat there; the sun was almost up, and that sky looked like a dark oil paint. She got up off the boat dock and walked down to the other end of the beach with her head full of sadness. She saw flowers in the sand. She picked one up—a red rose—and put it back down. She wondered who would put flowers on the beach. She then turned around to head back to the beach house, and as she begins to walk, she saw her mother coming towards her with the morning sky behind her in full color.

"I'll never forget the look on her face when she saw me," Debbie began to tell Jason. "It was a face that I have only seen once on her, but have heard about many times through Stacie. It was enough to burn right through you, and when she got close she grabbed me by the arm and yelled at me. My heart broke that day, she had never yelled at me like that before, and then she raised her hand to slap me, but stopped herself," she told Jason.

"Why was she so mad at you? What was it that you had done?" Jason asked.

"...I was on the beach. I was in her place. That's what she said to me before she hugged me and told me that she was sorry for grabbing my arm like a rag doll," Debbie said. Her eyes were wide-open and glossy, as if they were windows into her broken soul.

Debbie told Jason that she had run back to the house with a sore arm, and a heart full of pain, but she knew that her mother did not mean to hurt her like that. Margaret never grabbed her like that again, nor did she ever yell at her. Debbie told Jason that her aunt and mother would walk that beach together all the time, so, in an odd way, Debbie could see why Margaret would say what she did.

Jason could not see why Margaret would get so upset over something like that, but he did not say anything. He knew that was no reason to pull a little girl's arm and yell at her like that just because that beach held fond memories of a loved one.

Jason softly asked Debbie if she was sure that that was the only time her mother had handled her like that or raised her voice at her. Debbie fell into a long thought before answering his question.

"No...there was another time," Debbie said, now thinking of the new memory that had been locked away in her mind for some time.

Debbie had happened to notice that Margaret was not wearing the gold necklace that her and father had bought for her on her thirty-sixth birthday. Debbie was only nine-years-old at the time. It was a lovely gold necklace with two stones in the pendant; one was diamond, and the other was a ruby.

"She yelled at you for asking why she wasn't wearing it?" Jason asked with a shocked look on his face.

"Yes, you could say that," she said as she looked at his face. "She said if she wanted to wear it, then she would, and if she didn't want to wear it, then it was her choice, and no one else's. She then yelled out, 'so leave me alone! Just leave me,' and she walked out of the kitchen and into father's den, slamming the door aggressively behind her," Debbie told Jason.

Jason's face still held a look of shock. Not knowing what to say, and not believing that Margaret would holler at her own daughter over something so petty, Jason could not find any words to say that would ease the hurt. He held her in his arms hoping to console her. Debbie in turn hugged him with that feeling of security that his arms always provided. All Jason could really feel was the lingering warmth of her sister's love.

Debbie in no way felt like Stacie, but Jason closed his eyes and caressed her arms. Jason could almost smell Stacie's hair as he brushed the palm of his hand down the back of her head, and as he ran his fingers through her hair it felt silky to him. His notion to touch her at this moment was wrong; his judgment was off, he knew he had to withdraw his hands from her body along with his loving arms before he touched her in the wrong way.

"What is it, Jason? Can you hold me just a little longer?" Debbie asked.

"I don't want to go too far, and make you feel unhappy," he told her without realizing that he had already gone too far with her sister, and that alone would make her unhappy if she were to find out.

"What are you trying to say? That I don't want you to touch me? Jason, it's okay sweetheart, just hold me like you were doing."

Jason did as she wanted, and held her tightly in his arms as they sat on the sofa. And as they sat there, they talked about things that only held happiness.

9

Warmth rushed through Jason's ears as she kissed at his neck, and as he kissed at hers, the warmth intensified. His hands fondled her large breast as he held her firmly from behind in his arms.

"Jason," Stacie said as she placed both hands flat on the bed and both feet on the ground.

"Stacie," Jason called out as he cupped her breast once more and softly rubbed her light pink nipples. It was then that they made their way under the covers; Stacie moved on top of him like she had done the last two times they had played this forbidden game of love. Jason saw it as love because he had feelings for her, and to him it was not about making love; it was about much more than love itself. Everything about her was so sweet, and everything she did for him when they were not in bed together was caring and thoughtful. Jason could still see that shy person in her even though she was no longer shy towards him, and that was where her sweet personality dwelled. Jason was in love with that side of her as well as her outside. As far as his feelings for Debbie went, he was starting to forget that he even had any for her, even though he had held her just two days ago.

After they made love, they talked and held hands. Stacie asked if he would like to sit in the tub with her and hold each other. She had asked in a voice that was so soft that he could not refuse—not like he would refuse her anyhow—and so they went into her spacious bathroom and prepared a nice warm bubble bath for two.

Jason was the first to slide his already steamy body into the hot water. Stacie then eased herself into the hot bath and merged with Jason. She rested her wet body up against his chest under the white fluffy bubbles. He held her as they talked, and as he listened to her, something came to him, something that he had never thought of before, and something that made him really think. He told himself that Stacie and Debbie were nothing alike, and even though they were not like one another, there was always a way to tell if two people were related to one another. Jason thought of his own brother, and of how different the two of them were. He remembered how mindless he was to think that way about Debbie and Stacie, and that he was just like those mindless people that viewed him and his brother as the same person. They were so different; he saw now how rude it was to think that about Debbie and Stacie, but it was true.

Jason held Stacie even tighter and began to kiss her. Jason only wanted Stacie in his thoughts. He wanted to push Debbie out. Without realizing it, he had almost succeeded in ejecting Debbie from his thoughts. Stacie made all that possible; she also made Jason feel happy—happy like the way he felt the first time he met Debbie. He knew that soon he would have to head home, and a part of him just wanted to stay with Stacie.

"It would be nice if we could spend tonight together, or any night, for that matter," Jason commented.

"It would, but it's too soon for that. I never want you to leave, but I know you can never stay for long," Stacie replied.

They would have to hold on to that little dream and hope for it to come true one day, but for now they would just have to hold each other in the moment that they both resided in.

Stacie's feelings for Jason were just as strong as his were for her, and they were just as wrong. Jason made her feel different, unlike any man she had ever had in her life. No man had ever made her feel this way.

Stacie's thoughts were engulfed with images of being embraced by a man; the very same man that was holding her in that hot water, but the water, as hot as their act of indiscretion, was now cooling down a little. Steam still filled the room, and the large mirror and its thin black frame were now covered in a thin fog.

Jason and Stacie were relaxed, and they were comfortable, even as Stacie rolled onto Jason's chest to face him. Stacie observed the way his eyes examined her as she moved in the water—this was not the first time she observed his actions—and she knew from that gaze that his feelings towards her were not so different from her own.

"You're thinking of something, aren't you?" Stacie asked as she brushed away the wet hair from her face.

"I'm thinking of how lucky I a—" Jason stopped as a loud ringing pierced through his tranquil thoughts.

"I don't want to answer it. I want to stay here with you," she said as she kissed him.

It stopped ringing and then started again. Jason looked at Stacie, then over at the closed door. He knew that she was going to have to pick it up sooner or later. The ringing stopped for a minute, and then started to ring again.

"Well, I guess I have to answer it," she said thinking of what Jason was going to say before the phone had interrupted him.

She stood up, and Jason's eyes fell to her body again. She brushed away a thin layer of bubbles from her wet body, and she splashed water on herself to get rid of the rest of those bubbles that had concealed her naked skin. She watched his eyes follow her out of the tub and over to the towel rack, and as she did, the phone stopped ringing for a second. It soon started again.

"Who could that be? It must be important," she said, wrapping the white towel around her and rushing out of the bathroom.

Jason sat there and tried not to listen, but found it hard not to hear Stacie talking. She was not too far from the bathroom, and her voice flowed through the room to his ears.

"No. I'm busy. Later I have to be at a café for a photo shoot. Good bye!" Stacie said to whoever she was talking to.

Stacie returned to the still steamy hot bathroom. She knew that Jason had probably heard everything.

"Is everything okay?" Jason asked. The look on Stacie's face gave him his answer, and it was then that he realized that she was not coming back into the tub. Jason stood up and stepped out onto the flower bathmat as Stacie handed him a towel. As he dried himself off, Stacie ran the tips of her fingers over his stomach muscles.

"I'm, okay. You have nice abs," she said as she smiled up at him. She liked the fact that Jason was taller than her—by one-foot—and he could tell that she did by the way she always rested her head on his chest.

"That was my mom. She is coming over later. I told her no, but she said yes she was, and then hung up on me."

"I should leave then. I wish I didn't have to," Jason said as he placed his hand under her chin and tilted her head back so that he could give her a kiss.

Jason got dressed and thought about how he was about to tell her something before the phone had started ringing. He knew that he would have to tell her how he felt another time.

Stacie walked with Jason hand-in-hand to the door. They kissed one last time, and as she went to open the door she stopped.

"I think I know what you were going to say to me before the phone rang," she said, removing her hand from the solid brass door handle.

"You do?"

"Yes, and I feel the same way, but I want to talk to you about it the next time we are together, or when one of us says it, but not now," Stacie told him. They kissed goodbye and Jason agreed. Jason walked out into the hallway and turned back to see her slowly closing the door and waving goodbye to him. He waved back and then made his way down to the lobby and out the front door.

He was parked about three blocks down in front of a convenience store that was near a hardware store, a spot that was becoming his own. This was his new routine every time he came to see Stacie, which meant Debbie herself was forming her own routine of drinking every chance she got when Jason left her alone.

Jason always made it a point to go into both stores and get something that he needed, but for the most part, it was to make it look like he had not been in that area too long. He had done work just half a block away, so it was perfect if anyone asked what he was doing in the area.

His throat felt dry; it was warm out and he became thirsty after walking from Stacie's. The more his mind dwelled on it, the more he needed to satisfy that thirst. He went into the store and got a bottle of water. Jason bought a big bottle of *Evian,* and walked to the front of the store to pay for it. He stood just outside the store and took a swig of the cool refreshing water, and he noticed that he had forgotten his watch at Stacie's. He had taken it off before he slipped into the tub, but his mind refused to let him remember where he had put it down.

"*Shit!*" Jason said. He knew right then and there that he would have to call her and let her know that he had left his watch somewhere in the apartment. Jason called her cell knowing that Margaret would not be there yet, and when she picked up she was happy to hear his voice. Jason told her what he was calling about, and hoped that she would be able to find it.

Stacie detected the worry in his voice and assured Jason that she would look for it. She then made it clear to him that Margaret would not be staying long, and that she did not think she would see it anyhow.

Margaret had only been at her place once, and that was about two years ago; she had only come over because Debbie was with her.

Jason relaxed a little after hearing that. He didn't know what he was so worried for in the first place, because even if Margaret saw a gold wristwatch—a man's wristwatch—at Stacie's place, it did not mean that it was his. Jason was feeling the fear of getting caught, and that guilty feeling of what he was doing collaborated with his fear, making him worry about all the little things that came up. This came to him after he hung up the phone, and he thought about how he would deal with those new feelings. Jason knew he would have to do something—knowing that his infatuation for Stacie was never going to diminish—and he knew that he would have to do it soon.

Jason got into his truck and drove out onto Maple Drive, the street where he had done a landscaping job about a year ago. This would have to be his way home, because the main road was too congested. Jason turned right and headed home. He wondered if Debbie would ask where he had been, or if she was passed out in bed like the last time he had come home in the late afternoon. Debbie was anything but better; she was—in his eyes—rapidly going downhill. She was not even trying to get her problems under control, and he could not understand how she was drinking so much in the last three days. He knew that he would have to have a talk with her very soon, and it would be a discussion in which he would come out victorious. Jason would use her drinking and the refusal of her medication as the fuel to start his fire; it was the one thing he could exploit so that his intimacy with his new love would never die.

Margaret was close to Stacie's. She was on Maple Drive, about five minutes away, when she saw a black pick-up truck turn left onto a side street. Margaret caught a glimpse of the person behind the wheel, but it did not strike her until the truck had driven out of sight.

That looked like Jason. I wonder if that was Jason? What would he be doing down here? Margaret thought as she looked in the rearview mirror and questioned herself. She then thought of their lunch together and how Jason's black truck had 4x4 on the side near the rear, just above the tire. Jason had told her he'd redone it in airbrush. The two fours had been done in an Alice blue with dark blue trim, each a starburst. And the *X* had been done in a bright turquoise with white trim.

That was Jason. That truck had the same artwork; she knew that her thoughts were correct, yet it still did not give her the answer to why he was in the area.

Margaret parked at Stacie's and walked into the lobby of the condo. She was just about to use the intercom to call Stacie and tell her to let her in, when she saw one of her close friends.

"Margaret?" Betty said as she walked over to Margaret.

"Betty, how are you?"

"I'm, doing good. How is Richard? Has the doctor said anything new?" Betty asked with great concern.

"He's still the same, but we are all hopeful that he well come out of the coma before it's too late," Margaret told her as Betty called someone on the intercom.

"It's me, Kim," Betty pulled open the door and told Margaret to come up with her.

"He will be fine, just wait and see," Betty replied, "It takes forever to get into this place," Betty commented to Margaret

"I didn't know that your daughter lived here. Stacie lives here as well."

"That's nice. You're here to spend time with her," Betty said as they walked up to the man behind the computer.

"Yes," Margaret did not say anymore. She did not want to see Stacie, but she had to know something.

"My friend and I are her to see my daughter, Kim Day," Betty told the young man with a buzz-cut. Betty turned and gave Margaret a wink. Betty did not know it, but she had just done Margaret a huge favor.

Margaret just knew that Betty was going to ask her to come say hello to Kim, and if it had been any other day she would have loved to. Margaret wanted to spend time with Betty; after all, she had not seen her since the get together at the beach house.

"Maybe after you're done visiting Stacie you and I can get together and have an espresso. There's an excellent little place just around the corner," Betty suggested as they walked onto the elevator.

"I have no idea how long I'll be. Maybe I can meet you there," Margaret said. She knew full well that once she asked Stacie what she had come to find out regarding Richard, that it could take minutes for Stacie to tell her to leave.

"That would be okay. I never stay that long. Kim doesn't like long visits," Betty told Margaret.

"Stacie is the same way, and I know today won't be any different," Margaret said with a devious grin that revealed her true self.

10

Margaret walked the length of Stacie's floor until she reached her door, and before she knocked she looked around. Margaret liked the way the floor was done up; the small lights that hung over each door helped illuminate the floor more so than the four panels of lights that were in the ceiling. The carpet itself could not be ignored; its rich monochromatic blue made her feel like she was on the beach looking at the sky and the ocean.

Margaret took another moment before she knocked on the door; she could almost feel the ocean breeze, and hear and feel the cool water lap against her feet.

Margaret knocked on the door and then stood there waiting. She let a minute go by before she knocked again. This time she rapped on the door even harder. It took some time, but Stacie finally answered the door, and when she opened it, she was surprised to see Margaret standing there.

"Mom? I thought you were going to come over later in the evening," Stacie said, "and how did you get in the building? I didn't buzz you in." Stacie just looked at her as Margaret stood in the hallway.

"I do hope you're going to invite me in, or are we going to talk like this for the next little while?" Margaret said with that sharp tongue of hers.

Stacie stepped to her right and let her mother in. Margaret asked what she was doing, and if she had heard her knocking at the door or not. "I did, but I was busy."

"I see, well I won't take up much of your precious time. I just need to ask you something."

"And you couldn't ask me over the phone?" Stacie asked in the same sharp tone of voice that Margaret had used on her.

"I have my reasons. I'm just going to ask you. What do you know about your father's will?"

"Why? Has something happened to him?"

"No! Don't even think that," Margaret snapped.

"So, why are you even asking me about his will then?"

"Because, I want to know how and why you get everything, and why your sister gets nothing," Margaret asked her.

"I don't know anything about that. All I know is that you and Dad made your wills up together. The only reason I know that is because I overheard Dad one day on the phone say how he and his wife just did their wills together.

"Is that so. Daddy's little girl knows everything," Margaret remarked.

Stacie just stood there as if her feet were bolted down to the hardwood floor; she was stunned.

"I think it's time that you leave," Stacie said as she walked back over to the door. Stacie could almost feel those bolts being ripped out of her feet—breaking and tearing away at her bone and flesh—but it was only a feeling that hurt inside her heart.

"Thank you for stopping by Mom," Stacie said, standing by the door with her hand holding onto the door.

"I just got here and now you want me to leave?"

"I think its best that you do, and like I said, you should already know what's on Dad's will," Stacie told her again, still waiting for her to walk through the opened door.

"Stacie, I'm just trying to understand why he left everything to you, but if you don't want to tell me—"

"I told you, I don't know," Stacie reiterated.

"I'll just have to ask your sister then, maybe she will know something," Margaret said, looking at Stacie's long, droopy face.

"And if she doesn't, you'll still love her... won't you?"

"Why would you even ask me that?" Margaret replied with a blank face.

"I just want you to know that I'm not trying anymore with you, but I will always love you Mom."

"What do you mean by that: trying?" Margaret asked as she walked past Stacie.

"Dad wanted me to work things out with you, and so did, Debbie. You and I have not talked like Mother and Daughter in years. I even pushed myself in life so that you and Dad would be proud of me. I have a good career, and still I have you looking down at me. Dad has always been proud of me, so why can't you?"

"Maybe you should try a little harder, because I don't see when you have ever tried with me," Margaret said as she walked out into the hallway.

"I did. Remember, it was about two days ago. I called you, and you told me that you were busy, and I know you, Mom. It was late in the evening and you don't go out that late. I just feel that you didn't want to talk to me that night, and that's okay, but don't say I never tried with you," Stacie said, and then went to close the door.

"Are we not talking right now?" Margaret asked, placing her left hand on the door before Stacie could close it all the way.

"Not the way, Dad and Debbie would like."

"And what do you want?" Margaret asked, watching Stacie's eyes, hoping to see the answer in them before any words were spoken.

"I would like to have my mom back in my life, the one who once cared for me."

"I'm sorry you feel that way, Stacie. Maybe one day we will have that talk, but it will have to be when your father is back home, because that will be the only way we can talk about anything."

"If that's how you want it, then that's how it will be. I don't see what Dad has to do with the way you are towards me. You're not this way with Debbie," Stacie said.

"I'm going to say my goodbyes and leave it at that. If we ever talk it will not be about Debbie, it will be about you and I, so goodbye and we will talk soon," Margaret told her as she turned to walk away.

"Goodbye, Mom." Stacie closed the door and locked it. Her head was now filled with a million questions that were screaming out in her mind to be answered.

Stacie automatically thought of Debbie.

I wonder if she got a visit from Mom, or a phone call? When she called me she was not happy, and had just told me that she was coming over and then hung up on me. I wonder.

Stacie then quickly called Debbie, but she did not pick up.

"Pick up. Pick up. Pick up. Damn it," Stacie said as she let it ring a little longer before she hung it up.

Stacie took this time to think about her dad and why he would have a will with only her name on it. She really hoped Debbie knew something about it, because if Debbie had no knowledge of this, then Stacie would never know the truth until her father told her, and that was not going to happen anytime soon.

Stacie tried Debbie again, but this time she called her cell. Stacie should have thought of that before, but it never came to her; it was probably because her mind was trying to unravel what her mother had just shared with her.

"Hello," Debbie said as she answered. Her voice sounded different, as if it were off in the distance.

"Hello Debbie," Stacie said with no thought of how she had taken her new lover from her sister.

"Stacie?" Debbie asked in a low and groggy voice.

"Yes, it's me. Are you okay? You don't sound so good," Stacie asked.

"What do you want?" Debbie asked in a cold tone that expressed that she was not in the mood for talking.

Stacie had to ask. She had to know.

"Debbie, Mom was just here at my place."

"You two are talking?" Debbie asked.

"Yes, and no. She came over and was asking me all these questions about Dad's will. Do you know anything about his will?" Stacie waited for an answer, but it took some time.

"No. Why would I? I'm really tired, Stacie, and I can't think about things right now," she said as if her voice was fading away; it sounded like her phone was dying.

"Do you know anything? It's just odd that she is making a big thing about his will when she should know all about it. Why would she come and ask me about it? Just because everything is mine, if—" Stacie stopped herself right there, she was not going to even think it. "I...I just don't get it, that's all."

"I don't know. All I know is that they did their wills together," Debbie told her. "Together, as one."

"Together. They did it as one will, not two separate wills?" Stacie asked.

"Separate? Why would they do it like that? From what I know, it was done as one, like I just said," Debbie told her sounding a little clearer now. "Look, Stacie, I don't want to talk about this anymore. I'm not feeling all that great," Debbie said.

Stacie let her go, and then just sat there staring down at the phone. She knew that Debbie was not going to have that much information, but what she had said was helpful enough. She knew know for sure that her mother did not need to ask her about the will, because it was absolutely clear that she knew everything about it. Stacie wanted an answer to why her mother wanted to know things. Stacie remembered something that her mother had said.

Daddy's little girl. Maybe Mom wanted Debbie to have things, and for some reason Dad didn't. That could be it, and that would mean that Mom had no say in the will, or Mom was in full agreement with it.

"You have to sign a will before a lawyer," she told herself, thinking out loud.

Stacie grew angry knowing that her own mother would come over to question her about things she already knew the answer to. Stacie felt that she was asking her about the will to cover up for something else—maybe to see if Stacie herself knew what was in the will, and what was coming to her. Stacie would not know for sure why she was so inquisitive, so she dismissed it from her mind.

Stacie went to the washroom to cool her face with water, she felt as if she needed to cool down after talking to her mother. Stacie reached for one of her white facecloths, and as she did, she saw Jason's watch on the floor near the wastebasket. Stacie picked it up and held it with loving hands. Even though she had been in his arms no more than two hours ago, she wanted to be held by him again.

Stacie could see Jason in her thoughts, as well as Debbie's face within his; it was as if they were one. Stacie wasn't going to let Jason go now; she was falling in love with him. A part of her did not care how wrong it was; she had not been loved for who she was in a long time. Jason gave her that love that was missing from her life. He was not like the other men that had come and gone in her life, men that seen a beauty with long blond hair and large breasts. She knew Jason could see that, but he saw more. He had seen past that. This was the first time she'd been with a man and had not wished to be transparent, so that her inside feelings could be seen. Jason saw her for her and just how sweet she was. She knew he did. Stacie also knew that Debbie was not showing her sweet side; the way she was on the phone showed her that. Debbie never talked to Stacie like that—as if she was falling asleep on the phone—and the only time Debbie talked like that was when she had been drinking.

Stacie knew that it would only be a matter of time before Debbie was back in rehabilitation, and if that happened, would Jason stand by her side? He was not the loving boyfriend Debbie had first met, and he would have to dissimulate who he was inside for as long as he stayed with her.

Stacie did not want to see Debbie go through rehabilitation again, but it would be her own doing if she did. Stacie also did not want to lose Jason's caring and growing love towards her. Stacie would have to let things unfold between them without her intervening; her actions had done enough.

Stacie put the watch on her dresser; she would have to tell Jason that she had found it.

11

Only the sound of the hands on the grandfather clock could be heard through the large, empty house as Margaret sat in the living room; it could no longer chime every hour, because Richard had that part turned off, and now—only now—Margaret missed the sweet sound of those chimes. She had never been so alone in the big room before, and even though it had been about two weeks since Richard was rushed to the hospital, it felt like months in Margaret's mind.

Debbie was the only one that Margaret had in her life now until Richard woke up from his deep sleep, and whenever that day would come, Debbie would still be in Margaret's heart. Margaret knew that Stacie would be around as well—lingering around as long as Richard was alive—and that was something that would have to change. In Margaret's mind it was a simple equation, but it would break Richard's heart to find out that his little girl had *left* the family. At first, Margaret did not know how she would go about excluding Stacie from the family's everyday life.

Stacie never wanted to be near the family that much anyhow, so maybe things did not have to change at all. Margaret feared that Stacie knew things about the family's past, things that Margaret did not want her to know. There was no love for Stacie in Margaret's heart, that was clear, and if Margaret was going to use that hate to achieve what she wanted, she would have to do it soon. She had tried before, but failed. Margaret did not want to do anything too extreme, just something to get her out of the family, and that was when it hit her. It was so simplistic.

I should invite Debbie and Jason over for dinner, she thought as she got up to use the phone. The thought in her head was controlling her movements; perhaps it would be her little angel that she would act on.

There were secrets swimming around within the family that Debbie did not even know about, and even though every family had their skeletons, it was Margaret's responsibility as a mother to keep the girls safe—keep Debbie *safe*—from the ones that were deep in Margaret's past.

Margaret called up Debbie and could not wait to hear her voice; being all alone in that house with only your thoughts to keep you company was a lonely way to start the day. Debbie picked up the phone. Her voice was a little rough, but not as hard as it was when she had talked to Stacie earlier.

"Hello, Debbie, it's Mother. How are you?"

"Hello, I'm…okay. I was just resting," she told her as she swung her feet off the side of the sofa. They felt a little like soft pasta, but still had feeling in them. Enough feeling that she felt her right foot strike a cooler bottle that had falling out of her hand to the floor. She quickly shoved it under the sofa, not knowing the time of day, and fearing that Jason would notice it if he came home suddenly.

"Just had a wonderful idea," Margaret began to say as she switched the phone to her other ear, "How would you and Jason like to come over for dinner?" Margaret asked, unable to tell that Debbie had been drinking.

"Jason isn't home yet, but that sounds nice. I'll ask him as soon as he gets in," Debbie said, dropping her head forward and rubbing the back of her head with her left hand. She sat up and looked at her hand; there was no glittering ring on her finger, and if she kept drinking there would never be one. There was still time to stop; it was not too late.

Debbie would have to see this for herself, but if she could not see it, then she would risk losing Jason.

"Debbie, you still there?" Margaret's voice shook Debbie out of her daydream.

"Yes, I'm here."

"So are you going to ask Jason when he gets home?"

"Yes, and then I'll let you know," Debbie told her.

"I just thought of something funny. If you come for dinner, I will have seen Jason twice today. I saw him as I was driving down Maple Drive, on my way to Stacie's. He must have had a job down that way, or maybe he has a friend on that street," Margaret said, waiting to hear Debbie's response.

"I'm not sure if he knows anyone out that way. Did he see you?" Debbie asked as she sat up straight and tried to gather herself.

"No, he didn't see me, and I didn't think to honk at him at the time," Margaret grinned at what she had just told Debbie.

"I know he has been busy with new jobs, so he's doing a lot of running around," Debbie said in his defense, and then asked, "Why did you go to Stacie's today? You never go out to see her." Debbie wanted to hear it from her mother's own mouth.

"I just wanted to talk to her regarding something about your father. I have a feeling that you already know, and if you do, why ask?" Margaret said.

"I just wanted to know. I just wanted to hear it from you," Debbie told her. "So, it's true? You both did your wills together," Debbie asked.

"Apparently so, but it's not done the way I would have liked it. Debbie would you mind if we discuss this some other time?"

"Sure," Debbie said knowing deep down that later would never come. "I'll call you back and let you know if we are coming or not."

"I love you both," Margaret then said, suddenly.

Debbie took in the words, but could not swallow them.

"Both? What do you mean?" Tell the truth, Mother I won't think any less of you."

"The truth. I love you more than anything on this blue earth. I don't need to say anymore then that, so please don't ask. You must know by now that we are a family that is different from the rest. Sometimes you can't change things, Debbie. I know that you want me and your sister to talk, but it will never be the way it should be," Margaret then said goodbye and left Debbie in a world of wonder.

Debbie felt that she was trying to tell her something important without actually saying it. Debbie's head was no longer throbbing, but it was still weak from trying to understand that mind-bending conversation.

Debbie lay back down and slept for about an hour. When she awoke she made a cup of coffee and waited for Jason. He walked through the door at around five, and was unable to tell that Debbie had been drinking again. She did not seem unsteady on her feet, nor did her voice sound different; the only thing that he could tell was that her mood was getting worse.

Jason asked her how her day was, and she told him that it was fine, and would he like to go to her mother's for dinner.

"That would be nice," Jason said.

"Good. I'll call her and let her know that we are coming," she told him, and then asked, "Busy at work? Are you?"

"Yes, we have a new layout we're working on, and we are trying to get it just right."

"So you were at the studio all day?" Debbie asked with her mothers voice in her head.

"Well... not all day. I went out for some last minute supplies," Jason told her.

Debbie did not ask any more questions. Debbie knew that if she did, Jason would wonder why she was asking so much about his day, and that was the one thing she never did.

Debbie took a hot shower and got dressed in a black dress she bought in Paris years ago. She waited for Jason outside, and when he came out wearing one of his dress shirts, she thought of how lucky she was. She had this thought before and ignored it. She had talked to him about the drinking; it had been two days now without taking her pills and drinking, and she knew now that she could not do it on her own like she had thought.

It felt like time went by so fast as they sat side-by-side in the car, and before she knew it, they were almost there. They had not spoken to one another the entire time as they sat in the car, and she felt Jason slipping away because of her problems.

"I would like to talk to you later about what I'm going through," Debbie said to him as she contemplated what was going on in his mind.

"You're absolutely right, we should talk later. I can tell your moods have been up and down, and it's because you're not taking your pills, but that something we can talk about later, he said in a bold tone of voice as they pulled up to the mansion.

Debbie said nothing as she looked up at the tall black Iron Gate; she knew that it would be a talk that she did not want to be part of, yet it was a talk she had requested.

"You grew up here?" Jason asked as he gazed up at the light brown stone house, and the black olive rooftop. It was an L-shaped house with large Victorian windows. There was a long garden that lit up the front of the house with life, and lush vines that climbed the right side of the house all the way to the roof.

"Yes, Stacie and I grew up here, and we went to school right down that street. It's one of the top schools up here; it's a private school," Debbie said with a little hate in her eyes towards his boldness. Jason looked at her and smiled.

Margaret opened one of the large, floral, white front doors and stepped out into the warm air. She waved to Debbie and Jason as she held a drink in her left hand, and then started to make her way down the dark gray stone steps. Those half-moon steps were beautifully done, and as Margaret walked down them, Jason could not help but stop and look at the wall of hedges that guided him to the front of the house.

"We should get something like this for our front yard," Jason said.

"You really want something like this in the front of our house?" Debbie asked taking hold of his hand, and for that brief moment they both forgot about their problems.

"I care about you, Debbie," Jason said unexpectedly, just as Margaret drew near.

"I know you do, and I care for you as well," Debbie said.

"Jason, Debbie. I'm so glad you could make it," Margaret said, giving them both a hug.

They all went inside and stood in the long hallway; the inside was as impressive and luxurious as the front entrance.

"You have a beautiful home, Mrs. Whiting," Jason said.

"Thank you, Jason, but this is only the hallway. You should tell me how you feel after you see the rest of the house," Margaret said to him. "Debbie, show Jason around and I'll prepare us some tea, and a little snack."

"Yes, mother," Debbie, said as she and Jason walked hand-in-hand down the hall.

"We'll be sitting in the family room," Margaret called out as they turned into the library.

From the library they made their way upstairs and Debbie showed Jason her old childhood bedroom, and he could not believe the size of it. It was almost as big as the drafting room outside his office, and that was a large room. She then showed him Stacie's old room, and her mother and father's room as well. All three rooms were so beautiful, and in a way, it made Jason think of his own childhood home. He did not have a large bedroom, but he had what Debbie and Stacie never had growing up: love from both parents. He did not know the Whitings, but he could tell that *love* was not what the family was built on. Jason could see that through Stacie alone, and Debbie had issues that she should not have had as a child, and he knew that a child that had a lack of love would develop problems that would manifest in their adolescence.

"Over here is my Father's study, and down the hall is the music room," she said.

"The music room?" Jason asked.

"Yes. You can sit and listen to music, or play on the grand piano. Would you like to see it?" Debbie asked him.

"Sure!"

His eye fell immediately to the glossy and checkered hardwood floor; it was in two levels. The grand piano was on the raised level, and it stood there as black as a moonless night. The shadow it cast on the floor was as dark as nightfall. It seemed hard to look at, but even harder to look away from. Jason could remember playing the piano in school, and not once did he ever come across a piano that looked as exquisite as this one. It was exquisite, and it felt as cold as a dark winter night.

Debbie showed him two more rooms before they headed back downstairs to the family room. They had their coffee and talked the hours away; Margaret told Debbie and Jason that they were going to love the dinner that Gina was preparing for them, and that the salads she had made herself. Gina was Margaret's maid. She only came in three to four days a week, but agreed to make dinner for her because Margaret was having guests.

"I hope you like salmon, Jason?" Margaret asked as she reached for her tea and waited for his response.

"I love salmon."

"That's good, because we're having lemon and blood orange grilled salmon, with truffle-butter rock shrimp," she said.

"It sounds delicious. I love shrimp as well," Jason also told her.

Before they knew it, Gina had come into the family room to tell Margaret that everything was almost ready.

Margaret had made a veggie-salad, a pasta-toss, and a Greek-salad.

"I love the salads, and the salmon," Jason said.

"Thank you, Jason," Margaret said, "and how about you, dear, do you like it?"

"Yes, I love it," Debbie said.

Margaret then thanked them both for coming to dinner, and said that it had been hard these last weeks alone in the house. Margaret told them that she could not wait until the day when Richard would come walking through the front door. She asked if they were going to the hospital soon, and Debbie said that they should.

"We haven't been in some time," Debbie admitted.

"How about tomorrow?" Margaret asked, looking over at Jason.

"That's okay with me, I'm *off* on weekends," Jason said.

"Tomorrow it is, then, that's final. Tomorrow morning," Margaret said without taking her eyes off Jason. She then commented, "Speaking of '*off*' I saw you today in somewhat of a hurry, taking off down Maple Drive."

Jason peered up at Margaret from the bowl of Greek salad.

"What? I'm sorry, I…"

"Today, at around—well the time doesn't matter. What matters is that I saw you, and I was going to honk, but by the time I realized it was you, it was too late. You had turned off of Maple Drive," she said.

"I had to run out and get last minute supplies at the art store. I'm sorry I didn't see you. I would have waved if anything," he told her before he ate some of the salmon.

Debbie knew right then that Jason was not being honest, because the art store was nowhere near Maple Drive. She had been there once before, and back at the house he had told her that he had gone for supplies, but he did not say where. She slowly pressed her thumb into the tip of the sterling silver fork until it bled. She could feel her rage, but she was motionless and speechless as the hurt from his lies went deeper then that self-inflicted fork wound. Debbie wanted to know right then and there, at that moment, where he had gone, and where he had gone all those other days. She knew that she may never know, but she knew that he was leaving early some mornings to go somewhere.

After dessert they all sat back and talked for at little while longer. Debbie and Jason left at around ten, and thanked Margaret for dinner and the—soon to end—pleasant evening.

They did not speak to one another as they drove home, and as much as Debbie wanted to express all her pent-up rage, she did not unleash it within the car. Debbie opened her purse instead, and popped open a small pill box and took two anti-depressants.

Jason could see out of the corner of his eye that they looked different in color. He asked what they were for, but she did not reply. As soon as they reached home, Debbie went straight to bed. She felt so sluggish, and she just could not keep her eyes open any longer. She said goodnight, pulled the covers up over her and fell asleep within minutes.

"Goodnight," Jason said, as he got ready for bed himself. He looked at himself in the mirror as he prepared for bed and Jason could almost see something in his eyes, something dark and sly.

Her purse. How many pills is she on? Jason thought. He finished up in the washroom and went downstairs; at first he could not see where she had put her purse. He had seen her come in with it, so he knew it had to be here somewhere. Jason went over to the closet and opened it; her purse was hanging up with her coat. Jason opened it and searched it. Within a minute he withdrew two different pill bottles. One bottle was for (Prozac), and the other was for (Celexa). Jason could see that two different doctors subscribed them to her.

"Two?" Jason said to himself under his breath as he held a bottle in each hand, and wondered what was going on in her mind.

It was on the tip of his tongue to ask her about her pills as he opened the blinds to let the morning sunlight in, but he did not say anything as the sun filled the bedroom; he could not bring himself to do it after seeing the mood that she was in. There was no need—*so he thought*— to upset her over something that she was dealing with as best she could. Jason watched how she sat up, and turned towards the window; it was like watching someone look at the world for the first time.

Debbie held her hands out in the warm sunlight, smiled, and then said, "Good morning, Jason. You're up early."

"I know. I couldn't sleep. And it's not that early," he told her as he looked over at the alarm clock. "It's ten-to-seven." That was not early for Jason.

"That's good. Good for you. Well it gives us time to eat before we go to the hospital," she said as she slid her feet into her slippers.

Debbie walked downstairs as if she was in the home of a hostile stranger; the banister felt smoother, almost like wet rubber. Sunlight filled the house like a church, yet it had passed through smaller windows. Debbie thought she was dreaming, but it was no dream; it was just the feeling of not being drunk and light-headed.

Debbie made a pot of coffee for Jason and herself, and suggested that they should eat at the hospital.

"Okay, but if we leave now we're going to be there rather early, and your mother probably won't be there yet."

"She gets up before us. She'll be there," Debbie told him.

"Okay…let's go," Jason said as he walked to the front door.

Debbie got ready as Jason started the car. Debbie stepped outside and closed the door, and as she went to go lock it, she felt a sharp pain in her thumb. She looked at what she had done to herself, and felt a little different about the day that started out so bright.

It didn't hurt when I did it, so I'm not going to let it hurt me now, she thought as she turned the key and heard that inevitable clicking sound of the door locking.

Debbie hid her thumb from Jason; she was ashamed of it, but more ashamed of herself. She hoped Jason's eyes saw her and not her thumb; she did not want to answer to it.

It took no time at all to reach the hospital, and that was a good thing, because she was so worried that he would see her thumb. They both satisfied their hunger with a ham and bacon sandwich, a banana muffin, and a second cup of coffee. They then made their way up to the room.

Something came to Debbie; she had never thought of it until just now, and it was something that could happen to her if she was not careful—she would have to keep her thumb from her mother as well. If Margaret saw it she would worry, and think about the past (that time when Margaret had found her on the living-room floor).

They stepped off the elevator and could see someone walking towards them with their head down. The person was walking rather fast, and as they got closer, Debbie could see the person's face.

"Stacie? Hi," Debbie said.

Stacie glanced up at Debbie with raging eyes, and said, "Hello, Jason." It was then that Debbie turned to him as if she knew something was between them.

"It was I that said hello to you, not him," Debbie said seeing that something was obviously wrong with her.

"Are you okay? What is wrong?" Debbie asked, not remembering her promise, and not allowing Jason to get his greeting in edgewise.

Stacie's furious expression had formed a mask on her face that spilled out words in anger.

"No, I'm not okay! And do you want to know why? Because I came to see my father," she began to say as bystanders looked on, "and found out that my bitch mother was here!" Stacie said as she began to walk away. She was so livid; Debbie could see it in the way that she talked. Stacie had said *mother,* and she had never could Margaret 'Mother' before; it had always been 'Mom.'

Debbie went after her and grabbed hold of her left arm. "What is it? What happened?" she asked.

"You didn't tell me that she was coming here today. That's what happened. Remember? I asked you, and you told me that you would let me know when she was going to be at the hospital," Stacie said reminding her.

"Sorry. I forgot!" Debbie was starting to feel that anger growing deep inside of her. She knew that she would have to get away from Stacie before her temper got worse.

"I'm sorry too. I'm sorry I fucking came here today," Stacie replied as she walked away from Debbie and Jason.

"Don't get all pissed off with me, Stacie! I said that was sorry. I forgot. Maybe you should grow up and start working things out with her!" Debbie shouted out as Stacie got onto the elevator.

That night back at home Debbie sat in bed thinking of Stacie as Jason turned in his sleep.

I hate how she makes me feel, she thought as she slowly lay down, resting her head on her puffy flower pillow. *I told her that I forgot. I told her that I was sorry. She should be apologizing to me.*

Debbie's eyes became heavy with sleep and closed as she turned towards Jason; her slumber would be short.

12

Jason was abruptly woken in the early morning by a car revving its engine. He slowly opened his eyes all the way, and as he got up to see who was on the street, Jason found that he was alone; the left side of the bed had been somewhat made, but not done very well.

There were no lights on in the hallway, or downstairs, but the bathroom light was on with the door closed. Jason closely observed the soft glow of light at the bottom of the door for movement—shadows that came and went as they pushed and broke away at the line of light—but nothing caught his eye.

"Debbie. *Debbie!*" Jason called out. He went to see if she was okay. He swung the bathroom door open all the way; letting it hit the wall and echo out a low thud through the empty room.

Jason stood in the doorway for a moment and scanned over the bathroom. His eyes had not yet adjusted to the bright lights of the room. There was nothing out of place; the only thing was that the lights were left on, but he could not shake the feeling that something was wrong.

Jason went downstairs hoping that she was on the sofa, but she was not, and when he looked outside he saw that her car was gone. It was only then that the realization of that car revving its engine was Debbie, and the thought of her passed out somewhere faded from his tired mind.

He felt like a fool as he sat down on the sofa. Thinking that something was wrong was so insane, but he really had thought something had happened to her.

It was still dark out and Jason had no idea where she had gone, and in a way, he did not care. However, he cared about her. He did not understand how he could, but he did.

Debbie took the back roads to Stacie's. Debbie had to talk to her. She had gotten a call from her mother who had told her that there had been some movement with her father. He had moved his left hand a little when the nurse was tending to him, and that was a good sign that he would come out of the coma, yet they could not tell her exactly when.

Debbie was a little unsure if she should go to Stacie's to tell her about their father, but it was more then that. Debbie wanted to talk to her about the other day, and the way they had spoke to each other. Debbie wanted to do this now, while she was calm and thinking about her father.

Stacie was not at home. Debbie called her on her cell, and Stacie picked up. She told Debbie that she had no time to talk, and that she was on her way back home. Debbie told her that she was at her place, and that she would wait for her to arrive. Debbie waited for some time, and felt that Stacie was taking her time just to try to avoid talking to her. Debbie then saw her coming up the path; she held that look on her face, the one from the hospital.

"Hello," Debbie said as Stacie walked up to her. "There was some movement in Father today. Mother just told me, and so I thought I would come and tell you."

"I already know about Dad. Where do you think I just came from? You're up early, Debbie. You came here to talk to me about Dad? Well…did you?"

"No. I wanted to talk about the other night. Can we talk inside?" Debbie asked, as Stacie walked passed her.

Once inside the apartment Stacie told her that she was not in the mood, and for her to say what she had come to say, and then leave.

"If you didn't want me to talk, why would you agree for me to come up with you?"

"Would you have left if I had asked you to?" Stacie asked. Debbie did not answer. "...I thought so."

Stacie told Debbie that she was letting her past catch up with her, and that she could see it coming. Debbie knew that this was true, and that she was right; she needed to get help, and fast, before it was too late.

"What was it that got you so upset the other day at the hospital?" Debbie suddenly asked, without warning

"Just Mom, being Mom. Nothing new," Stacie said, not wanting to see Debbie's face anymore. Stacie at one point had to look away, because it was as if she could see Jason's face inside of Debbie's. Stacie knew that it was her guilty conscience that was playing with her mind, and making her want Debbie to leave even more.

"Can you please leave, Debbie? We can talk about this another time when things in your life are more under control," Stacie said, looking dead into Debbie's eyes.

"What are you trying to say?" Debbie asked.

"I think you know what I'm getting at."

"You're absolutely right, I do," Debbie said walking past her as she headed straight for the washroom, and then asked, "May I use your washroom before you kick me out?"

"If you must, but don't take long," Stacie said as she stood holding the apartment door open.

Debbie used the washroom, then washed her hands, and that was when she heard Stacie's phone ring. Debbie turned the water and the bathroom lights off and could hear Stacie talking to someone; it sounded like work. Stacie was asking about her photos, and if they would need any touch-ups.

Across from the bathroom was Stacie's bedroom, and it looked as nice as the rest of the apartment. In a way, it made Debbie think about her life and what she was doing with it. Stacie lived a very nice lifestyle, but she had worked for everything she had. Debbie lived just as well, if not better, and had never worked a day in her life. Margaret made sure of that, she would never allow it, not her Debbie-angel. Debbie peeked in and took a quick look around, and saw matching oak night stands with matching lamps. Debbie heard Stacie hang up the phone, and just as she went to turn to walk back to the front door, she saw a gold watch on the dresser. Debbie could see that it was a man's wristwatch with a black face—too big for Stacie to wear—and that told Debbie that Stacie had a man in her life.

"Are you still in the washroom? I have to go out," Stacie called out to Debbie.

"You have to go somewhere?" Debbie asked.

"I just told you, *I have to go out.* Did you not hear me?"

"Going to see someone?" Debbie asked wanting to know if there was someone special in her life.

"Goodbye, Debbie," Stacie said as she put her shoes on and balanced herself with one hand on the open door. Debbie walked past her and out into the hall.

Stacie locked the door and ignored Debbie as she brushed by her and walked straight to the elevators; she was acting so cold towards Debbie, and it was so clear to see. Stacie waited for the doors to open, and when they did, she told Debbie that she could take this one or wait for the next one.

"Are you feeling okay?" Debbie asked.

"Yes, I'm fine. I just don't want to be near you right now," Stacie replied.

"If that's how you feel, then you take it," Debbie said stepping back from Stacie. Stacie's coldness towards her was making Debbie upset, but not in a sad way.

On the way home, Debbie thought about what her mother had said at dinner, and about the art store—*"Fine-Line"*—and how it was nowhere near Maple Drive. Debbie pulled on the steering wheel as she began to get mad. She asked herself why Stacie was acting that way towards her. She could hear her mother's voice over and over again in the middle of her head.

MAPLE DRIVE . . .

MAPLE DRIVE . . .

"I saw him coming down Maple Drive."

Debbie's mind raced on and her mood worsened as she drove home. It was then that she thought of Jason's watch; the one his grandfather had given him. Debbie could remember Jason telling her about it soon after they started dating. She knew how much that watch meant to him, and he wouldn't just wear it to work, or out to the store. She knew now what her mother was trying to insinuate. Debbie knew her mother would not have said it to hurt her.

Debbie thought about the night when Jason had told her what Margaret had asked him when she was on the phone at the restaurant, and maybe she had asked him that because she saw something. Debbie didn't want to think of it while she was driving; she couldn't bear the thought of what it all added up to.

She reached home and just sat in the car for a couple of minutes. As they rushed through her, those dark thoughts had no mercy on her unstable mind. Debbie went inside, and went straight to the washroom. She had not had a pill since dinner at her mother's the night before, but she had a drink before she went to Stacie's. She had kept a small, unmarked bottle of whiskey in the glove compartment of her car, and she was careful not to get pulled over while she was drinking from it.

Maple Drive. Gold watch. Stacie. GOLD WATCH . . . STACIE . . . MAPLE DRIVE, Debbie's thoughts said the same list of words over and over again. She still needed to know for sure if that list in her head meant anything at all, or if it was just her dwelling on what her mother had said to Jason.

I saw him on Maple Drive; the art store isn't even near there.

That was not all Margaret's voice had implanted into Debbie's head. Margaret's voice played a big role in all of Debbie's other thoughts¾Debbie's thoughts sounded very similar to Margaret's voice.

It was as if Margaret was behind Debbie, pushing her along. Debbie went through Jason's things and could not find his gold watch. She slammed the dresser drawer shut, and that was she heard Jason come in through the front door. Debbie ran out of the room and down the stairs and saw him go into his studio.

"Jason!" She called out to him.

"I just came back to get some things, and then I'm gone," he told her.

Debbie told him that she had to talk to him, and that it would not take long. She asked him again about Maple Drive, and why he was there the other day; she was beginning to sound repetitive.

"I told you already," he said going around the room picking up the things he needed.

She quickly reminded him about the other night when he told her mother that he had been to *Fine-Line,* saying that it was close to his work place. Debbie confronted him, saying that if that was true, then there was no need to be on Maple Drive, unless he went to see someone near there.

"I don't know anyone on Maple Drive, or anywhere near there. All I know is that I go down that way to get gas then head to the store to grab a paper," he said, looking at the face of the girl he had first met almost a year ago.

She questioned him about the gold watch that his grandfather had given him, and how maybe he had left it at his girlfriend's fancy condo. Jason shot back at her, and asked her what the hell she was talking about.

"Stacie! I'm talking about Stacie! Debbie yelled out at him in a sobbing voice.

"Stacie? Now you're sounding just like your mother. I don't even know where your sister lives. You have never told me, and I have never asked, and I never talk to her unless I see her at the hospital with you right there!" Jason yelled back at her.

Debbie didn't know what to say to that. She thought that she had made a mistake in thinking that he would do something so dirty and low, and that maybe Stacie did have a man in her life.

Jason made it clear that if she was going to talk like her mother then she could go and live with her, because he was not going to live like this, and he did not want to go through this with her on her off-days. He told her that he knew that she was still drinking, and then he asked her when she had last taken one of her pills. Debbie just stood there, unable to move; she was frozen, and unable to speak. What she had feared was now coming to life right before her eyes.

"Get out," Jason said in a low voice. He had thought about saying it for so long, and now she had just given him all the reasons he needed to let his words fill her ears.

"You want me to leave?" Debbie asked, looking at him with wide eyes and shock across her face.

"Yes. Get…out," Jason's eye did not move as he looked at her, and his face held no feeling, "and when you stop drinking and start taking only the pills you're supposed to take, then, and only then, we can talk about you coming back here to live if you wish."

"I may never come back. Would you even care?" Debbie asked, still unable to move.

"I'll be back in three hours, and I would like for you to be out of my house by that time," Jason said as he picked up all the paper and tools that he had came home for. He walked by her and out the front door without saying another word to her.

Debbie went around the house that she had called home for so long, and gathered up all her clothes and personal things. She put all her things in the back of her car and headed up to the beach house. There was no way she could stay at the estate, not with her drinking again; she had friends, but she couldn't think to tell them what was going on in her life, let alone ask them to help her out. Debbie knew that it was the beach house that would be her new home, or nothing.

13

Debbie had been gone no more then two days, and within that time Jason had been with Stacie once more.

Stacie was upset and needed to talk, but most of all she needed the comfort from Jason's loving arms. That comfort turned to lust, and that lust into their forbidden passion that was now their dark taboo.

Jason told Stacie that he had told Debbie to leave, and that she was the only person he wanted to be with. Stacie couldn't help but feel responsible for what she had done towards Debbie, but she wanted Jason from the first time she laid eyes on him, and Debbie, in a way, had pushed him away with her drinking. That was how Stacie saw it, even though an awful feeling ran through her body. Stacie knew that Jason would have left Debbie sooner or later, because Debbie was gradually falling apart each day.

Stacie told Jason that Debbie had come over to talk to her. Stacie said that she wasn't going to watch Debbie throw her life away over her drinking, like she had done before. She told Jason that Debbie listened to everything that Margaret told her. It all started when they were young, Stacie explained.

"I think she was yelled at a couple of times, and it hit her hard, because she was already upset about things," Stacie told him.

Stacie drifted back and remembered a mother who used to love her and show her things like painting, making little paper animals, and learning how to handwrite in cursive.

Stacie held Jason tight and shards with him the time when she was young and learned how to write in cursive before Debbie could. Even though Debbie was older than her, Debbie just could not get the hang of it. Debbie would try and try, but just couldn't do it.

"Maybe my father is wrong, like I have always thought," Jason began to say, "he always used to tell me that left-handed people are smarter then right-handed people, but I think that's all 'B.S.'"

Stacie told him that it was not crap, and that her aunt Peg was left-handed.

"She was smart, but somewhat of a bitch to me," Stacie said as she made an unpleasant face.

"Is your mother right-handed? Debbie said something about it one time," Jason asked as he moved in closer to her.

Stacie told him that she is right-handed, but she gave up trying to show Debbie how to write in that style, so aunt Peg had to show her whenever she came over to visit.

Jason asked why her aunt Peg would show her, and how could she show Debbie how to write if she was left-handed. *Perhaps a left-handed person could teach a right- handed person how to write; it could be done,* he thought. He knew very well that it could be possible, but to him it just didn't seem right somehow.

"Because my aunt Peg was ambidextrous, I think. I was young and I have a difficult time remembering everything about her, and you don't dare ask Mom about her sister. Mom took her death hard, that's when it all changed between me and her, but I don't say that to anyone, even though I just did … to you. I have never even told that to Debbie," Stacie said with a tear running down the side of her cheek.

Jason held her tight and kissed her, and as he did, so he thought of those two old picture frames at the beach house. Jason tried to remember what Margaret was wearing and what she was doing. He knew that there was something odd about the pictures, but he couldn't remember, and then it slowly came to him like a dark cloud passing in front of the sun and slowly giving light back to the world.

In the pictures Margaret was holding a pen in her right hand, and in the other picture she was holding the pen in her left hand. Jason knew that it was just a picture, and that Richard was holding onto her shoulder. Jason knew that the photographer could have told her to pose that way, so that Richard could stand on her right side, but he couldn't really say for sure. All Jason did know was that the photos looked a little odd to him, and nothing more than that.

Jason felt that he should say something to Stacie about the pictures, and when he did she just looked at him.

"Why do you feel that's important? Even if she is using both hands in those photos, it doesn't mean a thing. My grandparents once had a portrait done, and my grandfather was holding a cup in his left hand, but he was right-handed. It was the young artist that told him to switch hands, because of the lighting off the cup, or something. She will always hate me, no matter what," Stacie told him.

"She doesn't hate you, Stacie. She just needs to get to know you all over again. She has pushed you out of her life as a child, so she never got the chance to know you as an adult," he tells her.

"Maybe you're right, but I could never talk to her about it. She is so different. In a way she reminds me of aunt Peg, and that's sad, because I love my mother. I... I," Stacie stopped and thought about what she had just said.

"What is it?" Jason asked.

"Nothing. I just had a thought, but it was nothing. It's gone now. It was just a stupid thought, something that could never be."

Jason and Stacie spent their first full day together, and for the first time in a long time Stacie felt happy and was falling deep in love. Jason felt the same, and talked to her about one day moving away from this town. Stacie told him that would be the best thing for the both of them, and they both knew the reason why.

Stacie felt that if they did move, she could somehow work things out with Debbie—without her having any knowledge of her secret love with Jason—and still keep in contact with her father. She would be away from her mother, and that would be for the best. Margaret did not want her around anyhow, so it seemed right. Maybe her moving away would bring them all closer together. As abnormal as that sounded to her, it was probably the best idea.

They both talked into the night—mainly about their dreams, their feelings for one another, and the moment that they were within—it was a relaxed conversation that could easily set the mood for love in anyone. Stacie had all the lights turned down low, and even though there was no soft music filling the air, they were pleased with their warm surroundings.

Jason and Stacie both had that look in their eyes that they had held before, and Jason did not say anything. He knew that he should wait until the time was just right… like now.

"Stacie," he began to say as she turned towards him.

"Yes, sweetheart," she replied before their moist lip came together.

They kissed for what seemed to be a long time. They then looked thoughtfully at one another before Jason spoke.

"I love you, Stacie. I love you so much. The first time I saw you… I just. I—"

"I know. I was there. I felt it too, but I just didn't know how to say anything afterwards. I even felt it that time when we both stood in line for coffee at the hospital. I love you too, Jason," she said as they kissed, and then made love.

Jason spent the night and held Stacie close to him as they slept within each other's embrace. Their warm bodies under the satin sheets helped them to fall into the world of slumber. It would be in that place that Jason's warmth would feel like a cold winter's chill, and her hands would slowly leave his body to be by her own side. Soon, she would turn onto her side and have no contact with her new love, and it didn't take long for that coldness to return. Dark images hid behind gray clouds in her mind.

Stacie moved in her sleep as she saw her mother walking from the beach to the blue and white beach house. Stacie followed her through the thick mist that covered the landscape, and parts of the ocean and trees. For some unknown reason, the mist could not form over sand, and was only allowed to cover certain things: the things that Margaret would never care about.

Stacie walked towards the beach house, and as she did she looked down at her hands. It was hard to see them under all that dense mist, and she knew right then and there that she must be part of the landscape that Margaret did not care for. Stacie put her ghostly hands down by her side and kept walking towards the house. Even though it was about four yards away from her, it seemed much further away.

Margaret opened the door and walked into the dark house. Inside, Stacie could see Margaret head up the stairs into a dark rolling mist. It looked like large rolling waves off water, and it made the house feel darker, colder, and uneasy.

As Margaret reached the top floor, Stacie could see her taking a key out of her left pocket and using it to unlock a bedroom door. Stacie walked up the stairs to the open door and looked in. She could see Margaret looking at a book that was resting up against a glass jar. Stacie could not see what was in it, the book that is, and as she stepped into the room, Margaret turned and looked at her. Margaret started to walk towards Stacie and through the mist that covered the bedroom floor. Margaret was yelling at her, but no words could be heard.

Jason could feel Stacie moving from side to side, and trying to say something. He sat up, and just by watching her; he knew that she was dreaming about something unpleasant.

"Stacie. Stacie," he called out to her, hoping that she would wake up. He did not want to shake her while she was in a deep dream. His mother had once told him to never do that to someone while he or she was in the dream world, but she never told him the reason why.

Jason always thought it had some sort of relation to when you frighten someone; too much shock to the mind—or heart—was traumatic, but that was just a theory.

"Stacie," he called out one more time.

Just then she snapped out of her nightmare, and said nothing as she lay there.

"Are you okay?" Jason asked with great concern.

"Yes, I'm fine. It was just a weird dream," she told him in a low voice that was still a little groggy from sleep.

Stacie fell back into that deep sleep, but this time her dreams were peaceful and filled with bright images.

Once again, Jason held her in his arms as he himself fell asleep, and even though they would wake up in four hours, it was a tranquil period of time for the both of them. Stacie dreamed of Jason, as Jason dreamed of her. Jason knew all too well that that was something lovers went through. He had once dreamed about Debbie, but it was not the same as how he dreamed about Stacie.

Debbie had an even harder night than her sister. She had fallen asleep rather early, and woken up with pain shooting through her head, and arms that begged for some blood—they held only tingling fuzzy energy and she was unable to lift them at first. She sat up not even wanting to move, or think of anything. Her heart did not want to bear any more pain over Jason, and her mind refused to listen to Margaret's voice talk about Maple Drive. Margaret should have just asked why he was so close to Stacie's place, because that was the impression that Debbie had stuck in her head.

Her hair looked matted on one side and frizzy on the other side. Debbie did not care how she looked. She sat in the dark living room with the curtains closed. She did not want to see the sunrise, because it would only hurt her eyes to let the sun fill her new world of darkness.

She did, however, allow herself the pleasure of hearing the sound of the ocean, and the seagulls that called out to one another as they flew back and forth above the length of the beach.

Debbie got up and made herself a pot of black coffee hoping that it would help her through another day, but it never did; it really only helped with clearing her head.

Debbie thought she would have seen her mother by now. She had been at the beach house for two days now, and she knew that Margaret came up to the beach almost three times a week to walk in the warm white sand, and to be alone, and to leave flowers for the ocean to reach out and take.

She's going to love seeing me here. Then she'll ask me how I got in, Debbie suddenly thought as she dropped two sugar cubes into her coffee. It should have been black, but Debbie had to taste a little bit of sweetness in this beautiful house that was turning into a place of sadness. She looked at the coffee cup; the flowers lined in gold around the cup looked dirty and old. Debbie then looked at the table, that long sofa, all the paintings around the living room, and even the windows. Then she looked away. At first she did not understand why she was shooting her eyes around at all these different items, but then it came to her.

I'm in a box. Just like before. I have put myself back in a box. Four walls, and a lid… and a floor, she knew that her thoughts were true, and that she had to get out of this place.

She did not want to live at the mansion, and to try to get her own place in the state that she was in didn't seem right.

Debbie was taking her pills a little more now, but still it was not enough. There were times that she would be so unhappy, yet then there were times that she would just drink and fall asleep, and forget all about her pills. At home she would have her mother to remind her, and she knew that she would be there for her, but she just wanted to be alone right now.

On the wall was an old clock in the shape of a swordfish that Richard had bought when the girls were young. Debbie thought about getting up and out of the house for a bit after seeing that it was midday; after all, she had been away from the rest of the world for two days now.

She thought about going home—her home—and trying to talk to Jason. She would let an hour pass, so that she could get a couple more cups of coffee in her before she got behind the wheel of her car. Debbie hoped she was doing the right thing, and she hoped that he would hear her out, because she loved him and she needed him by her side to get through this. She never once considered what she would do if he didn't take her back, and she never thought of doing it all on her own. She didn't need Jason to get through this; all she needed was herself to set things right in her life––a life that felt as if it were crumbling beneath her feet.

14

Bright light filled the entrance of the poorly-lit underground garage as Stacie opened the large metal door to the street above. She made her way up the ramp and turned right onto the street. Stacie headed off towards the beach house. She had to see what Jason was talking about.

Stacie thought about her night with him as she turned onto Main Street. It felt right to wake up with Jason by her side, and to be in his arms. They even had breakfast together for the first time, along with a cup of coffee—cappuccino for her.

Stacie had told Jason where she was heading, but she didn't tell him about her dream. That was the one thing she kept to herself; she only told him about the things that had mattered to her, those things that moved her soul whenever she was near him.

Jason made her feel wanted, and not just for her beauty like all those hungry camera eyes she stood in front of for most of the day. He made her feel wanted, needed, loved, for the person within. She didn't know if her thoughts were right—she would never know just how right they were.

Jason looked past her beauty and saw just how sweet and kind she really was. Still, it was her stunning looks that had helped him to see those qualities that she kept hidden behind her sheepish light blue eyes. It was those same eyes that hadn't noticed Debbie parked across the street from the condo. Debbie was not just out in the open for all of Main Street to see; she had parked beside a Rogers's cable van that partially obscured her, yet still allowed her to have a full view of the front of the building. Debbie did not want to stay in that spot for long; it made her feel like she was doing something wrong. Debbie watched the front doors open, and saw all the happy faces that came and went.

They look so carefree, she thought to herself as she watched a small group of people come out of the building.

Debbie tried to call Jason at home to tell him that she was coming over to talk, but there was no answer. She left him a voice message, and told him how much she loved him. Debbie hung up and tossed the black cell phone onto the passenger seat. Minutes passed, and she wanted to leave, but something inside of her told her to wait just a little longer. Just then, one of the doors of the building swung open and Jason emerged into the sunlight, and into Debbie's vision.

Debbie's heart slid down into the hollow emptiness of her stomach as she closed her eyes in disbelief. Her thoughts impersonated her mother's voice and began to say the name of the street over and over again in the back of her throbbing head. It didn't stop until she threw her hands up and covered her face. Her hands quickly became saturated with tears. Debbie pulled her hands away from her face, and she could not see Jason anymore. For a moment, she thought it had all been in her mind, but then she saw him walking down the street out of the corner of her eye. She watched him walk about a block before he got into his truck, which was parked in front of a store. Debbie sat and waited to see which way he would go, but she already knew which way he was going to take home. *Maple Drive.*

Debbie followed him until he reached the corner of the street she had called home for almost a year now. Now it would be Stacie's home along with everything else that came with it. Debbie couldn't help but think of her father at that moment, and how he had left everything to Stacie. How Debbie wished he would wake up from his coma, so that she could ask him why. Debbie's head was spinning with sorrow and dismay.

Jason went inside and got a drink. He saw that the phone had one voice message. He played the message back and tried to contact Debbie to tell her not to come over, but she did not answer her phone. Jason stopped and thought about calling Margaret. After all, that was were Debbie was going to stay—so he thought—but when he called the house, Margaret told him that Debbie never showed, and that she did not know where she was.

Where did she go? Jason thought to himself. He didn't care at this point, but he still wondered. He said goodbye to Margaret and tried Debbie's cell again. This time she picked it up. Jason quickly asked her where she was, and said that he would come down to see her so that they could talk.

Debbie told him that she didn't want to see him, and that she knew everything. Debbie began to sob, and each cry echoed out over the phone.

"What are you talking about?" Jason asked. "I don't understand. Would you just calm down, and talk to me."

Debbie tried talking, but found it hard as she struggled to push the words out of her mouth one by one. Jason was able to make out what she was trying to say. He heard her say beach house, and, no more… and Stacie.

"No more… what? Debbie are you at your mother's beach house?" Jason didn't get a reply. "Is Stacie with you?"

"My sister! Why my sister!" Debbie yelled out in an ear-piercing cry.

"I told you already, that if you're going to talk like your mother, then you can go live with her!" Jason hollered back, and then said, "Don't bother calling back. Do you hear me? I can tell that you have been drinking."

"You don't have to worry about that, because I'm fucking leaving you! And I'm never coming back! I hope my sister was worth it! I never thought you would ever do anything to hurt me like this, but I was wrong," Debbie said through her tears of pain.

"You don't know anything, Debbie. You're not thinking straight, so if you want to leave, then leave, and never come back."

"Goodbye, Jason," Debbie said in a low, weeping voice as she hung up.

Jason stood there holding the receiver in his hand. His heart held no feelings or remorse for Debbie's cries.

"She is worth it," Jason said as he slowly hung the phone up.

He thought about what she had said. Debbie had mentioned something about the beach house. Jason knew that if Debbie went up to the beach house and saw Stacie there that she would start yelling at Stacie in her drunken state.

Jason tried to reach Stacie on her cell phone right away, to warn her that Debbie was on her way up to the beach house, and that she knew about them, but Stacie did not answer.

Debbie sat in the car, slamming the side of her fist against the door handle until she thought she could feel pain in her wrist. Debbie felt no pain in her wrist, but her heart felt pain. It felt like it had just been slit open, and that pain was greater then anything that she had ever felt before.

Stacie's pretty little face flashed on and off like a dim light in a dark room inside of Debbie's head; the young pretty face was teasing Debbie as she started the car, but it didn't stay in her mind for long as the sound of the engine pushed it out. Debbie didn't want to see Stacie's face right know. Debbie knew that she would release her anger and yell and swear at her, and then walk right up to her and slap that pretty face so hard that it would turn candy apple red.

Debbie sat there for a moment. She looked down the street one last time before driving off. She couldn't go back to the beach house, not yet, so she headed to her mother's.

Debbie was not sure if she should look for comfort from her mother, but she couldn't go anywhere else for love or support. Debbie knew that Margaret was the only one that she could turn to; she was the one person that had always been there for her.

15

Stacie immediately felt a cold chill wash over her as she stood in front of the beach house; that unpleasant feeling almost pushed her to the ground like an on-coming wave, but she braced herself against her car until she was able to proceed onward.

She had never been to the beach house before on her own. She thought back to when she was in school, and how she used to get into the beach house when her and her father would wait for Margaret to get all her weekend bags out of the car. Stacie would have to use the bathroom, and so she would head round back and get into the house before them, but that was because the back door was always broken.

Stacie wondered if her mother and father ever got around to getting it fixed after all these years. She made her way to the back of the beach house and saw that a new door all together had been put in, something she failed to notice at the party. Stacie was now unsure of how she was going to get in. She knew her mother kept every door and window locked, but Stacie would try the front door regardless. She knew that it would be locked, but what if she was to leave after coming all this way only to find out later that it had been unlocked.

Stacie slowly climbed the white and blue steps to the front door and turned the doorknob, and as she did, it slowly left her cold hand and swung open. Stacie walked in and closed the door behind her. It was dark and cool inside; almost every window was covered up. Stacie walked around and opened the drapes to let more sunlight push away the darkness. It was only then that she felt some warmth in her body.

It had been warmer under the soft covers with Jason, and even though she did not think of it, that thought sat in the back of her mind as she looked around the house. She could see cups on the coffee table, and a plate on the floor that still held remnants of someone's meal. Stacie couldn't pull her eyes away from the state of the living room, and she knew damn well that it was not her mother who had left that plate of unwanted food on the floor.

"Debbie?" she said under her breath. "It has to be Debbie."

Stacie was right, she knew that it had to be her, since Jason had thrown her out. Stacie knew that *Mother* would never have told Debbie to go to the beach house. She would have told her to stay with her at the estate.

Margaret never let anyone go to the beach house without her presence, and Stacie knew that if Mother found out that Debbie was living at the beach house, she would be furious with her.

Stacie did not know where Debbie had gone, or when she would be returning, and she did not care. Stacie wanted to talk with her and work things out, but she wanted Debbie to have a clear head before they walked down that road. From the way that the living room looked, it was clear to see that Debbie was falling deeper into her past life.

Stacie went into the next room and looked around. There was nothing out of place, and it didn't look like it had been lived in. Stacie moved through the silent room and felt as though the walls had eyes that were following her every move. She walked over to the window; it was the same window that Jason had stood at on the day of the party. Stacie could remember looking up at him, and waving. She felt the same way now that she had felt then, that feeling of wanting to be with him, and the inability to show it.

Jason's voice was in her head, and it was calling out to her. Stacie could almost hear him talking about the pictures, the ones of her mother, and as she turned to look at them, Jason's voice left her mind.

Those frames no longer shined in the sunlight, and even though the room held more light then the other room, the portraits couldn't help but look dull and dark. She looked at the pictures and saw what Jason was talking about. It didn't mean anything to her. Richard always stood to the right of Margaret, and that was just something he did, something he did all the time. In one picture, Richard was standing to Margaret's left, and to Stacie it still didn't mean anything to her. She knew that he might have been told to stand there by the photographer.

There was a lot of hope in her heart that she would find something to help her understand why her mother had questioned her about the will, and why *she* was the only one on it. Stacie knew that the answer to why she was the only one on the will wasn't going to be found in those two old pictures, but she hadn't come all this way just to see them. She wanted to try and find an answer for those other questions that splashed around within her head, questions from her dreams that needed acknowledgment.

Stacie was a little unsure of what she was searching for, but she would know what it was when she came across it. Her eyes looked over the candlestick holders, but nothing jumped out at her. Stacie made her way upstairs. She moved slowly—there was little light to guide her because the light overhead was burnt out.

Darkness filled the upstairs hallway, and the air seemed different somehow. Stacie could tell that the air had changed; it was colder, but she didn't know how that could be.

No sunlight. That's how. I just have to open some rooms, and then some windows, and then it won't feel so cold up here, she thought as she slowly made her way down the hallway, opening the bedroom doors as she went.

It didn't take long for the afternoon sunlight to fill the hallway and push out more of the darkness, but it didn't push out that coldness, and it wouldn't ever be able to. The chill that Stacie felt was all her own; it was the cold from being in the beach house, and it was the fear of her mother finding out that she had been there without her permission.

Stacie knew what room she was going to look in first, and it was only because she hadn't been in that room in years.

Debbie and her had their own rooms at the beach house, and they each had their own washroom. Stacie walked through her bedroom. It all came back to her, and it was nice to feel and to see things that she had not seen or felt in years.

All her dolls still sat on her canopy bed, and her white dressers stood as tall as ever; the gold handles still shone as bright as they did on the day her father brought them up to her bedroom.

Stacie turned and stepped back out into the hallway, and then turned towards her mother's room. She walked up to the door and turned the knob—she knew that she had to see what was in there, but it was locked. She began to wonder if it had always been locked, and if so, why? She knew deep down that it was to keep Debbie and herself out of the room.

"Damn it," she said, thinking of how she was going to open the door. Stacie thought about picking the lock, but she had never done that before; she had never even seen it being done. She noticed that the door didn't stay closed all the way. It moved inward about a quarter of an inch, but it was just the way the door was; it was still locked, but that little bit of space gave her some hope of getting into the room.

Stacie went back downstairs to the main floor, and then down to the basement. She looked around her father's small workshop, and at first she didn't see anything that would help her get that door open. Stacie would be crossing the line with her mother if she followed through with her thoughts, but she did not care anymore. She needed to know if there was anything in this house that would tell her about her father's will. That door kept her from seeing the inside of that room, and so she began to believe that there was something up there in this beautiful beach house.

Under the workbench was where he kept all his big tools. There was a saw, a large power drill, a crowbar, and in the back were cans of paint that had their individual colors running down the sides of them.

The color had stopped halfway down, as if it was frozen in time, just like her. Stacie couldn't move when she saw the tool that would help her open her mother's bedroom door. She stood there looking at it, knowing that once she opened it there was no turning back. If she found something in Margaret's room, then she could use it to back up her impulsive actions, but if she didn't find anything, then her mother would have all the more reason to hate her.

She reached for the crowbar and felt the coldness of the steel as she picked it up. She held it up with both hands and felt just how heavy it was. Stacie held it in both hands the same way she would be holding it when she was ready to open the bedroom door, and she did so just to get a feel for it. She also did it because she would have to be quick; she had no idea when Debbie would be returning, or worse, when Margaret would show up for her long walk on the beach.

Stacie quickly rushed upstairs with the thought of someone coming in and catching her in the act. She did her best to ignore her anxiety as she stood in front of the bedroom door. She placed the crowbar just above the handle, and pulled it towards her. It cracked, but nothing more. She kept pulling, and as she did, the doorframe began to crack as well. There was now a little more space for her to work with. Stacie repositioned the crowbar; this time she placed it right on the strike plate and pushed—not pulled—as hard as she could. Just then the door popped open, and as it gave way, Stacie fell forward, dropping the crowbar.

Stacie stood upright, and then stepped back; the air was a little stagnant. She caught her breath and went back into the room; she wasted no time in opening all the windows. Fresh air began to circulate through the room, making it easier for her to breathe.

Looking around the room was like flipping through an old Eaton's catalogue. Everything in the room was outdated, but still in great shape for its age. In the far corner of the room stood a tall dresser--that was where she would start her search. Stacie still wasn't sure that what she was looking for would be here; she felt now that something like a copy of the will, or some kind of attachment to the will would be at the Estate. Stacie ignored her thoughts, and kept rummaging through the drawer that held old clothing.

As she went to push the second last drawer back in, she felt it hit something. Stacie removed the drawer and reached into the dresser to feel around for the obstruction. She pulled out an old brown folder. It was thick and stained—ring stains from a teacup, or something—and there were more then one stain on that folder. Some of them looked so faded that they were almost lost in time, and the others looked as fresh as the day they were formed.

Inside were old photos of her mother and father, but one photo stood out as she looked through them one by one. She had a hard time trying to look at it because it was so faded, it had been in water, and was crawling up at the corners. It was of her mother and aunt Peg, but Stacie couldn't tell who was who, not even all these years later. All Stacie knew was that her aunt was a hard woman, and that she had lived all alone.

Stacie put the drawer back into the dresser and then put the folder inside the drawer. She stood there for a moment thinking of how stupid it was of her to break into her mother's bedroom just to look at some old photos. She turned and looked at the glass closet doors—*sliding glass doors*—and it was as if she was back in her dream, but this was no dream. Things were as clear as day, and she knew that she was fully awake. She threw open one of the glass doors and began to go through it looking for whatever she could find. Within minutes she found something that was covered up with an old pillowcase. She could hear paper rustling around inside the pillowcase, but there was something else that was in there, something made of glass.

Stacie removed the unknown object from the old green pillowcase, and put it on the floor in front of her. Stacie's eyes were glued to the large glass jar that had a white ribbon tied around it. She took a closer look at it, and then moved away from it.

What is that? Is that hair? Is that human hair? Stacie's thoughts were correct.

Black hair filled the jar, and some of it was tied with white ribbon. Stacie didn't know what to make of it, but she knew she couldn't just stand there all day staring at it all. She put the jar back into the pillowcase, and pulled out all the loose sheets of paper to begin going through them.

Stacie could see that all the sheets of paper had no lines—just lines of bold writing—and that it was on colored paper. It reminded her of the paper that she and Debbie would draw on as kids, but it was not as thick. Stacie looked at a red sheet of paper that was on top of the stack, and it read:

Love you, Richard. I have always loved you. I know one day you will see the real me, that loving person inside, and not just the mirror image of the love you lost. You know who I am from our time spent not too long ago, but now you can get to know who I really am inside.

I love you, and I know you still hold deep feelings for me as well.

Stacie looked at another page; it was written on emerald green paper, and it read:

Miss you, my loving sister. I hope you can see that I love you, and that I try to be with you as much as I can. I will bring you flowers soon.

Richard has been there for me when I feel sad, but he is sad too, and looks at pictures of you. I know now that he really sees me, and when he holds me, I know he loves me so.

Stacie could not believe what she was reading, and her mind was having a hard time piecing it all together.

Why would dad look at pictures of Aunt Peg? Was Jason... right? Stacie thought as her stomach slowly turned. She forced herself to look through the rest of the letters for more proof. Stacie wanted to see something that held a name, or a date on it, but there was nothing. Stacie then thought that she hadn't looked thoroughly at the jar of hair that sat next to her covered up in that pillowcase. She turned to the pillowcase, and as she did the bedroom door slammed shut. Stacie dropped the sheets of paper as she jumped with fear. Stacie closed her eyes, gathering herself from the fear that rushed through her. Closing her eyes helped calm her and put her at ease again. As she went to pick up the different colored letters, she noticed that one of the sheets had a white ribbon attached to it. There were three letters on the ribbon—three characters that were upside down from where she stood. They were readable—and they spelled out the name PEG in gold. Stacie reached down and picked it up, and slowly turned it over and began to read it:

I'm so happy that I'm with my love, Richard. I love him so.

The rest of the paper held a photo of her father and at the bottom of the page it read: **Love from . . .**

It didn't say a name, but in a way it did. Stacie flipped the letter back over and looked at the ribbon one more time.

"Peg. Love from ... Peg," Stacie said as she felt cool air touch her lips, and kiss the sweat on the sides of her face and her neck. Her stomach turned a little more as that cool air turned into a cold shiver that slowly crawled down her back. Her numb fingers dropped the colored paper all over the floor again, as she turned to look over at the pillowcase.

She took the jar of hair out and looked at the ribbon; it was the same as the one on the back of the letter. Stacie examined it again, but this time she scrutinized everything in that jar until she saw something on the ribbon. The jar turned and turned in her hands, but all that hair made it hard to see if anything was on the ribbon. She tipped the jar forward so that she could look at the bottom of it, and that was when she saw the letters. It didn't spell out a name, but it didn't have to. In gold the letters read: MARGA— Stacie couldn't read the rest. There was dark hair obscuring the rest of the letters. Opening the jar and moving the hair so that she could read the rest of it was an idea, but it was one she couldn't bring herself to complete. Stacie knew it was a name. She knew that it was her mother's name, and she realized that it was also her mother's hair.

Everything seemed to slow down in Stacie's mind and all around her. The jar slipped from her hands and moved with great speed towards the floor. That jar hit the floor and shattered just as Stacie began to cry over the realization that she had grown up without a mother.

Things started to come together in her mind. Other things stood stark and alone, hungry for further answers. Her mind raced on as she moved the hair and broken glass with her foot—she still refused to touch it with her bare hands—until the ribbon could be fully read.

"Mom," Stacie said, as she thought of the woman that had played with her as a child. Someone that was more than a woman—a mother that loved her.

Stacie slowly made her way into the hallway despite her sluggish feet. Her face was blank, and her eyes a little red. She tried to put her thoughts in order, but couldn't. All she could think of was how she and Debbie were lied to all these years, and for what reason? Why? What was the reason? Must of all, what really happened to their mother?

"Debbie," Stacie said as her mind kept going through a checklist of questions.

She rushed to the phone to call Debbie, but the phone was dead. She hung it up, then picked it up again, but there was still nothing. In a way, she could see why the phone would be cut off--they were never here, and everyone had a cell phone.

"My cell," Stacie uttered under her breath. She quickly rushed downstairs and out the front door. She hurried as fast as she could over to the car, and retrieved her phone from her handbag. She struggled to get it out of that handbag, and when she did, she immediately called Debbie.

16

Margaret could only see sadness within Debbie's eyes, and pain within her face as she listened to her daughter's inner cries for love; heartache rang out with every word that followed Jason's name. Margaret comforted Debbie the best she could.

"Debbie, I know it hurts, but you have to let him go. You have to think of yourself. You're so beautiful, but look at what you're doing to yourself, sweetheart. You have to do what the doctor said. Remember the last time? You have to stay on the pills for at least six weeks before they start working."

Debbie couldn't think of anything but Jason and Stacie, and how all she wanted right then and there was to come face-to-face with them so that she could ask them how they could hurt her like this. Debbie looked like a woman who hadn't slept in weeks, and hadn't kept up her appearance within that time. Her lips looked whitish and dry, like dead snakeskin, but it was her red eyes that showed her pain. They were almost closed like crimson red shutter slats, but open just enough for her tears to fall through.

"She has done it. She has done it now. I tell you, she has done it now. I want her *out* of this family, and off the will," Margaret uttered.

Debbie turned to Margaret and said, " How can you think of the will after what I just told you about Jason and Stacie?"

"I'm so sorry sweetheart, but I'm just so mad at your sister. You can see that…can't you? I'm thinking of you. I'm always thinking of you."

Debbie leaned forward in the chair and hugged her mother. Margaret stood in front of Debbie with her hands caressing the top of her head.

Just then, Debbie's phone began to ring, breaking the tranquil moment between mother and daughter. Debbie slowly answered it without viewing the name of the incoming caller. She thought it might have been Jason at first, but when she heard the low voice on the other end, she knew right away that it was Stacie. Debbie stood up, breaking free from Margaret's loving embrace, and yelled, "Stacie how could you?"

Margaret's eyes shot up at Debbie's pain-filled face.

"Hang it up, Debbie. She's no good," Margaret said, trying to take the phone from her hands. Debbie turned away from Margaret and walked into the dining room.

"Debbie it's…" Stacie's phone cut out and then came back.

"Where are you, Stacie? I can't understand what you're saying."

"At…beach h—" Stacie's phone was almost dead. Stacie looked at the battery bar––there was only nine percent left; the reception was bad up there and didn't help matters.

Debbie hung up, she didn't need to talk to her any longer then she had to. She stuffed her car keys into her front pants pocket and started to storm off towards the front door.

"Debbie, where are you going?" Margaret asked as she followed her.

"I'm going to talk to her face-to-face."

"You shouldn't go when you're like—" Margaret suddenly stopped herself.

"Like what? Upset, or not thinking straight!" Debbie's face lit up with rage as she quickly turned and questioned her mother.

"I just don't want you to do something foolish."

Debbie didn't want to hear her talk anymore; she didn't want to hear it, because the words out of her mother's mouth were the truth.

"Debbie! Debbie, just take a minute to calm down."

"No! I'm going to talk to that fucking bitch!"

"Well at least tell me where you're going? Did she tell you where she was?"

"Yes. She said the beach. I think she is at the beach house," Debbie said. Debbie didn't have to turn around to know that her mother's face was probably on the floor, but it was too late to take those words back.

"Sorry, but that is where I'm going."

"You girls know how I feel about people being there when I'm not accompanying them," Margaret said as she looked at the side of Debbie's face. She saw a cold look in Debbie's eyes, and then asked, "Where did you go after Jason threw you out, Debbie?"

Debbie didn't answer her; she didn't want to, and in a way she knew Margaret already knew the answer, and fully understood it.

"We could go together," Margaret suggested.

"No, I'm going on my own," Debbie said, and Margaret could not help but feel Debbie's pain.

"I don't like this, but if you are going and you don't want me there, then you two can talk about your problems somewhere else," Margaret said.

"Fine," Debbie said as she walked out the front door.

Margaret would go to the beach house, but she would wait for a little time to pass. Margaret also wanted to talk to Stacie—a talk that would keep her away from the family forever.

* * *

There was a buzz that echoed down the halls of the hospital. The afternoon shift was getting ready for the long evening ahead of them. Some of the day shift lagged behind to talk and to hear about anything that may have happened on the off-shift; it was mainly gossip, and very little of it was work-related.

Minutes later, the rest of the day shift left for home, and the afternoon shift got underway. They always started off by doing their rounds, and picking up where the last shift left off. Most of it was checking up on patients, and seeing if they were okay. Some of them took pills that needed to be given every hour on the hour.

Nurse Kimberly had been on the afternoon shift for about a month now, and was a transfer from one of the smaller hospitals from outside the city. She had just finished giving Mr. Reese his pills, and was on her way back to the nurses' station when she noticed that there was a cool breeze coming from an open window in Mr. Whiting's room. Kimberly turned to ask one of the other nurses if it was supposed to be open, but the nurse did not know, and all the other nurses were off on their rounds. The one nurse that should have been there...wasn't.

Nurse Kimberly looked down the hall, but only saw Rachel. She was too far away, and Kimberly was not going to yell out to her or walk down to her. She could feel the cool wind whipping through the room; the air felt more cold then cool, and the dampness of the weather moved through her. Kimberly knew that it was only going to get colder—she had heard that it was going to rain all night before she left her home—so she took it upon herself to close the window. She walked into the room and closed the white-framed window, and then locked it. She turned and started to walk towards the door when she saw two nurses walk past the room.

Now they're around, Kimberly thought to herself as she walked towards the door and then out into the hall. Just as she stepped out of the room she heard someone call out to her.

"Nurse."

It wasn't a loud call, and it sounded close by. She looked to her right and saw that it wasn't a call from Nurse Tracy, who had just walked by the room with Nurse Tammy. She turned and looked at Mr. Whiting, and saw that he was looking right back at her.

"Nurse, could I have something to drink. Maybe something to eat?"

Kimberly almost dropped her clipboard and the little tray that once held pills, but she was able hold onto them. She wasn't scared; she was just shocked.

"Tracy!" Kimberly yelled. "Mr. Whiting is awake."

Nurse Tracy and Tammy quickly rushed to a nearby phone, and paged the doctor on duty to room #275. Tracy headed to the room herself, and when she reached it she saw that Kimberly was still looking at Mr. Whiting; Tracy also looked at him with shock.

He seemed to be fine. He was moving his head from side to side, and his speech was clear. He took in the cards that had been left by friends and loved ones, and the plant that Jason had replaced for Stacie.

"My wife, and my family," he said as he tried to move. "Are they here?"

"No. But they have been almost every day," Nurse Tracy told him, and then said, "Try to lay still, your body has been at rest for a long period of time, and your muscles are going to feel stiff. We will work on them soon."

"I… I can't remember how I got here, or what happened."

"You suffered a head injury at work, that's all I know," Nurse Tracy told him.

"You said I have been at rest for a long time?"

"Yes. You have been in a coma, Mr. Whiting, for about five weeks."

"I could hear people talking around me, but I couldn't say anything to them," he told her.

"That sometimes happens when a person is in a comatose state. You just rest now, and the doctor will be here soon," she told him.

"Will the doctor call my family?"

"Someone will call, don't worry," she assured him.

* * *

Margaret snatched her keys up from the end table and made her way through the house as quickly as she could. She was almost at the front door when the phone began to ring, and as she walked into the living room to answer it, she thought of Stacie. She hoped that it wasn't her.

"Hello," Margaret said as she listened to a low crackling sound. "Hello!"

"I know—" someone said before the other end cut out, and then came back, "Debbie will soon know…what I now know."

It was Stacie's voice, Margaret was sure of it.

"Stacie, what are you talking about? Answer me," Margaret demanded just as Stacie hung up.

Margaret slowly hung up the phone and stood there thinking of what Stacie was talking about. She didn't once think about her room; after all, it was locked. Margaret went to pick the phone back up to call Debbie to tell her to get her sister out of the beach house, but before she could, the phone began to ring again. Margaret was slow to pick it up.

"Hello!" Margaret's voice was hard and deep in tone as she yelled into the receiver thinking it was Stacie.

"Hello, Mrs. Whiting, please."

"Speaking."

"Mrs. Whiting, this is Saint-Vincent's hospital calling."

"Margaret almost fell into the wall knowing that they would only call her for two reasons: One––Richard had slipped into the darkness of death, or two––he was awake and free from his coma. Margaret sat down and switched the phone to her other ear. She asked, "Is my husband okay?"

"Yes. He is awake, and he has asked for you," the nurse told her.

"Thank God," Margaret said as tears of relief streamed down the side of her face. "When will he be able to return home?"

"It may take about a month. We can talk about it more when you come back to the hospital."

"Okay, I'll be down shortly," Margaret, said as she gleamed with happiness.

17

Debbie heard ringing in her ears—like chimes in a music box that play over and over—as she sat in her car parked in front of a small strip mall. The ringing stopped for a short time, but soon started up again. Debbie pushed the ringing out of her head as she held the bottle from the glove compartment with both hands. She watched the traffic go by. She had stopped off at a local pub, but found that the two beers she had at the establishment weren't enough to calm her down.

Debbie took a swig and then quickly put the bottle away and out of sight. Just as she did, a police cruiser slowly drove past her. Debbie looked down at her keys, and then started the car. She kept her eyes on the police cruiser as it drove to the end of the strip mall and stopped. She was just about to pull out of the strip mall when those chimes filled her ears again; it was her phone, and it had been her phone all along. She answered it, but at first she couldn't hear anyone on the other end.

"Hello...hello," Debbie said. She was about to hang up when she heard her mother's voice.

"Debbie, can you hear me now?" Margaret asked.

"Yes. Yes I can."

"Come back to the house as soon as you can. The hospital just called, your father is awake."

Debbie thought that her mother might just be saying that to get her to come back home. Debbie knew that she didn't want her to go up to the beach house, but perhaps she was telling her the truth. Debbie began to ponder how sincere her mother's voice sounded.

"He's okay?" Debbie asked in an odd way, as if she had a paper clip on the end of her tongue for a split moment; Debbie found it hard to form words, and Margaret picked up on it right away.

"Debbie where are you? You have been drinking, haven't you? I want you back home immediately."

"No. I have to talk to Stacie. I have to know why," she told Margaret in a voice filled with anguish.

"Debbie, you shouldn't even be driving around. Come back home, and we'll go up to the hospital and see your father together."

"I don't want Father to see me like this."

"Debbie, I don't have time for games. If you don't come back, I'm going up without you, and then I'm coming up there to get you," Margaret told her.

"Sorry, Mother, but I have to go. I'm almost at the beach house. I'll come back as soon as I can," Debbie said as she hung up and made her way out of the strip mall.

Debbie arrived at the beach house just as the sun was about to set; the sky was lit up, and even though six o'clock had come and gone, it still looked bright out. It was stunning and enchanting how the sun's bright yellow center reflected off the ocean's surface, and how its amber rays of light tried to hold onto the evening as the darkness came to take it away.

Debbie turned to the house and saw Stacie's car, but couldn't see Stacie, not yet. Debbie thought that she would have been out front waiting for her, but she was wrong. Debbie was so upset, that the thought of seeing Stacie's face made her think of things that upset her even more.

I want the truth, and then I'm gone, she told herself, but her thoughts were a little tipsy—just like her—and even though she could hear herself saying it within her mind, she didn't feel that way. Debbie really wanted to grab a hold of Stacie and give her a slap—a slap so hard in the face that it would echo out across the beach.

Debbie made her way into the house and called out Stacie's name, but there was no reply. Debbie could see that the back door was wide open, and that there was colored paper scattered across the hallway floor. Debbie saw a red sheet on the staircase. She picked it up, but didn't read it; instead, she dropped it and called out for Stacie one more time. Debbie then looked upstairs, but couldn't see if Stacie was up there.

"Stacie, are you up there?" Debbie yelled out as she headed up the dark stairs. She saw something on the floor at the end of the hallway— blue paper. She walked towards it, and that's when she saw that her mother's bedroom door was wide open. Debbie looked at the door and saw that someone has forced it open; the room was dark, and the soft glow at the window from the outside lights didn't help her see what Stacie had done to the room.

"Stacie, did you do this?" Debbie said to herself as a thought came to her: *Maybe someone broke in, and took Stacie. That could have happened, but if that did happen, wouldn't that unknown intruder have ramshackled the entire house?*

"Stacie, are you here?" Debbie called out as she went back downstairs.

Debbie walked past the kitchen and into the dinning room, then into the solarium. Debbie went to close the back door, but before she did, she looked out towards the beach.

Debbie began to feel—mostly fearful—that Stacie had just called her all the way down her so that she could be with Jason. Debbie stopped and thought. Jason had thrown her out, and Debbie now knew that it was so that he could be with Stacie. So, there was no need for Stacie to call her down here. Stacie could be with Jason whenever she wanted to without running into Debbie.

Debbie tried to get her head around the reason way Stacie had called her, but she just couldn't put the pieces together. She walked back into the dining room, and then into the living room with her hands hanging limp by her side; they were trembling. She felt so betrayed and just wanted to grab a hold of Stacie and shake her.

Debbie picked up one of the candlestick holders, and felt just how heavy it was. She put it back down from where she had picked it up, and became lost in her thoughts. She was trying to anticipate how she would get Stacie out of the house, and leave with her so that they could talk somewhere else, like Margaret wanted. Debbie didn't have to worry about it, because from what she could tell, Stacie was nowhere to be found.

Debbie headed back to her car, and thought: *Her car is here. What kind of a game is she playing?*

Debbie happened to turn and see something moving in the coming darkness down by the beach. Debbie walked around the side of the house when her phone began to ring; she quickly answered it.

"Stacie?" she says.

"No, it's your mother. Are you at the beach house yet?"

"Yes, and, Stacie isn't here. Her car is here, but I don't see her," Debbie told her in a voice that told Margaret something entirely different.

"I can tell that you have been drinking. I could tell it from the last time we talked as well. How many drinks did you have today, Debbie?" Margaret inquired.

"How is Father? Is he going to come home soon?" Debbie quickly asked, trying to avoid her mother's question. There was no real care for her father; Debbie was blinded by her own rage over Stacie.

"Don't worry about your father. You have bigger things to worry about, like finding your sister and getting her out of there."

"Tell father I said—"

"Forget about your father, and find your sister, do you hear me?" Margaret reiterated, but this time in a voice that was dark and low, and that held no more patience.

Margaret hung up. She wanted so badly to rush down to the beach house, but she couldn't leave Richard, not yet. Margaret stood outside the room just a little longer—almost in a meditative state, trying to imagine what was going on up at the beach house, and what Stacie was doing up there in the first place, and why Debbie couldn't locate her.

Cool, crisp air came off the ocean and rushed through Debbie's hair as she hung up the phone. She started down towards the beach. She knew it had to be Stacie moving around down there, and as she got closer to the white sandy shoreline that was now in darkness, thoughts of Jason began to fill her mind. Those memories fed her rage and helped it mature into hate, but there was something else inside of her, something other then those memories, and Debbie could feel it now in her gut. It was a feeling of sickness, but not just from her drinking; it was from the mixture of pills and alcohol.

Debbie stopped and took one look at the green grass that was obscured by the night, and it was then that she fell to her knees in pain. She had not taken a pill in two days, but on this day she had taken three before she left the beach house to go spy on Jason and Stacie.

That pain kept her down for a couple of minutes. It felt like someone was stabbing her just below the ribs, and as bad as it felt, she couldn't help but wonder why this pain hadn't happened to her in the morning. Debbie stayed down on her knees with her fingers clawing at the grass and sand; there wasn't much more she could do, so she thought, but she was wrong.

Debbie slowly placed her pointer finger down her throat and regurgitated. It helped relieve some of the pain, but only a little. She forced herself to repeat the unpleasant action, and found that she felt better after the second time. Debbie gave herself a moment to pull herself together before she stood up—she wanted to make sure that the pain in her stomach was gone before she started to walk onto the beach.

She wasn't going to let anything stop her from talking to Stacie, and hearing what she had to say for herself. She had come for the truth.

Debbie walked all the way down to the end of the shoreline, and saw Stacie standing at the end of the beach where the grass, sand, and trees came to an end, and met the ocean. Debbie couldn't help herself. She clenched her fingers into a fist, and slowly walked up behind Stacie.

18

Stacie stood in front of the dying flowers that Margaret had left in the sand. She envisioned those colored letters in her head, and as she read them back to herself, there was one that stood out: *I will bring you flowers soon… my loving sister.*

Stacie looked up at the dark trees that, in a way, were all looking down at her. She dropped her eyes back down to the flowers and stepped back. Stacie went over that letter in her head again and again, she was lost from time and space in her thoughts.

I will bring you flowers soon… my loving sister. **I will bring you flowers soon… my loving sister.** *I will bring you flowers soon… my loving sister.*

"O-my…God. No…it can't be," Stacie murmured as she took another step back. She threw her hands up over her mouth. She tightened her clasp as the wind blew from behind her, pushing her long hair in front of her face. She put all those years together at that moment. All those times that Margaret had turned her back on her, all those times that she was yelled at now made sense, but she still wouldn't know why. Why would her aunt Peg live her life as her missing sister? Perhaps it was to be with her father? If so, then that would mean Richard knew full well that Peg was not Margaret, perhaps the truth of Margaret's disappearance dwelled somewhere within Richard's mind. Stacie began to realize that this beach might be more then just a favorite place for her stepmother—Peg—to take long walks and relive her memories; it could be a burial ground for the missing. Did the flowers really mean that her birth mother was buried out her on this lonely beach? If so, why?

Stacie wanted to know, she needed to know, because there were things in her that needed answering.

Stacie thought of the bedroom, and of all the papers—*those letters*—and thought of how she never read them all. She found it hard to turn away from the flowers in the cool sand as she remembered the loving times from her childhood with a mother that showed her love just in the way she smiled at her. A tear ran down the side of Stacie's face, and touched the corner of her mouth; it was bitter. She wiped it away with the back of her hand as she lowered her head and turned to walk away.

"What the hell are you doing out here?" Debbie hollered at Stacie.

Stacie was suddenly startled as she looked up towards the unknown voice that cut through the cool night air.

"Debbie, is that you?" Stacie asked. "How long have you been out here? I called you—"

"Quiet, and listen. I came her to ask you something," Debbie began to say as she looked at Stacie, still clenching her fist. There was a lot of hurt and pain in Debbie's rough face. Stacie could see—even in the darkness of the night—that Debbie wasn't well, and that she had let her looks gradually fade away with every drink, just like she had before. Stacie could also see the savage look on Debbie's tired face as Debbie watched her the same way a lion watches its prey through the tall grass.

"Debbie, calm down," Stacie said not knowing what she was upset about.

"My Jason. How could you? You took him from me," Debbie said. Her eyes lost a bit of their rage, and for a moment, Stacie could see a small child in the eyes peering out from behind Debbie's long brown hair. They were filled of tears, and before Stacie could hold that image in her mind, those eyes quickly filled with rage.

"You took him from me!"

"Debbie, look at yourself."

"Don't speak to me. I want to know about you and Jason, and I want the truth."

"Debbie, what are you talking about? Just get a hold of yourself. I have to show you something," Stacie said as she tried to walk past Debbie.

"No," Debbie said grabbing Stacie by the arm and pulling her closer towards her.

"What the hell are you doing, Debbie? Let me go."

"No. You tell me to my face. Are you and Jason sleeping together? I know he's been to your place more then once."

Stacie couldn't say it. She knew she couldn't say it, because if she did, Debbie would be even more enraged, and worst of all, she wouldn't listen to what she had to say even if it was the truth. Stacie looked at Debbie's brokenhearted face, turned her head and said, "Mom is dead, Debbie."

"I can't believe you. You'll say anything just so you don't have to face me. Well, I saw Jason leave your building, and I think he has been with—"

Debbie started crying as she loosened her hold on Stacie's arm.

"Debbie, did you even hear what I just said? Mom is dead. She's been dead for years. I think aunt Peg has something to do w—"

"How could you? You are my sister!" Debbie yelled out as she pushed Stacie away from her. She did not want to hear anything that Stacie had to say. Debbie fell to her knees and punched her fist into the sand.

Stacie watched as the guilty feelings of what she had done tightened around her heart. It was hard to see her sister falling apart before her eyes, and harder to know that she had helped create Debbie's pain.

"Debbie," Stacie softly said as she went to help her up. "I have to show you the letters, then you'll see what I'm talking about."

"No. Just get away from me!"

"Look at you. This is why Jason left you, because of your drinking, didn't he?" Stacie asked, hoping she could slither her way out of her mistake by putting the blame on Debbie's drinking. Stacie no longer wanted to hold the responsibility of her actions.

"I called you because I thought you should know before anyone else, but I guess I was wrong. I should have just called the police."

"I know Mother is alive, because I talked to her not too long ago," Debbie said in a choked-up voice.

"That's not Mom, that's aunt Peg," Stacie said in a somewhat hard voice as she stood back up. "I should never have called you here. I'm sorry."

Debbie slowly stood up on legs that felt unsteady, and Stacie began to walk back to the beach house. As she made some distance between her and Debbie, it was then that Debbie called out to her, "You're sorry about what? What you are saying doesn't even make sense. Just tell me the truth…you bitch!"

Debbie wouldn't let it go as she followed Stacie all the way back to the house, making up ground as she went. Debbie was close to Stacie now, as they both made their way up the mound towards the beach house.

Stacie went into the dark house and straight for the letters, and then she went over to the stairs and picked up the rest of the letters. Debbie came in right behind her—still hounding her about Jason—and once more she grabbed hold of Stacie's left arm. Debbie pulled Stacie towards her, and began to yell at her, demanding an answer.

"Read them!" Stacie shouted back as she held the letters up as if to shield herself from Debbie's rage. "You read them, and you'll see what I'm talking about. Don't tell me I'm not making any sense. Go upstairs and look at the jar of hair from her closet."

Debbie slapped the letters out of Stacie's hand and said, "You're saying whatever you can come up with just so you don't have to face me, and answer me. Maybe I should call Mother, and tell her what you have done to her beach house," Debbie said, slamming her fist into the side of the wall.

"Call the police after you hang up with her, because she is not Mom. Read the fucking letters, Debbie! Just read them!"

Stacie picked the letters back up while keeping an eye on Debbie; she was watching for any movement from her fist, but there was none. Stacie tried to hand the letters to Debbie as she stood back up, but she wouldn't accept them.

"Father. What will he think when he hears what you have done to me? Hears about how you broke into Mother's bedroom? His little girl. You have always had his love. Always!" Debbie's face went a little pale as her child-like eyes returned to cut into Stacie's soul.

"Father loves us both, you know that. Why bring him into this? This is about aunt Peg," Stacie responded, still holding the letters as she slowly moved away from Debbie.

"Because he is awake," Debbie replied.

Stacie stopped and looked at Debbie; she was stunned, but could tell that Debbie was telling the truth. Debbie wasn't in her right mind, but Stacie knew when she was lying.

"She told you this? Stacie asked.

"You mean, Mother?" Debbie replied. "Yes, she told me."

"You know who I'm speaking of," Stacie said as she walked into the living room.

"I know you're trying to find a way to leave, and I was told to make sure that you are removed from this house, so leave…by all means, but not until I get the truth out of you," Debbie said as she moved in closer with those eyes that were now starting to fill with rage, and that were hungry for a confession.

Stacie didn't know what to say, or how she would say it even if she were to say anything. Debbie didn't seem that relaxed, and she feared that if she spoke the wrong words, that it would enrage her again.

"We got together and had coffee. He was worried about you not taking your pills; he could see a change in you. I called one night to talk to you, and he answered. He asked if he could talk to me about what was going on with you, and that was all. It was just talk. Nothing more. Jason just wanted you to stop your drinking, and have you take your pills," she told Debbie.

Debbie stood there for a moment and took it all in, and then she walked up to Stacie, and said, "Is that all it was? Are you sure? Why was he leaving your apartment minutes after you left? You can't answer that, can you? You can't, because you're a lying, fucking, little bitch."

"You're out of your mind," Stacie said. She went to turn and walk away, and just as she was about to do so, Debbie slapped her across the face. Stacie felt the sharp sting on her flawless face as she stepped back from Debbie.

"Debbie, stop it!"

Debbie was now blinded by the full fury of her rage, and she rushed towards Stacie yelling incoherently. Stacie pushed her away, but Debbie was taller and by far stronger, and Stacie knew it.

Debbie struck Stacie in the face and punched at her wildly. Stacie's lip split open, and she fell against the table that held all the candlestick holders. She used the table to break her fall, and some of them fell to the floor.

"Debbie, stop! Please stop!" Stacie pleaded with her, as she tried equally hard to restrain her, but she couldn't.

Debbie pushed Stacie again, and then reached for whatever candlestick holder she could grab a hold of from the table, and she hit Stacie with it. Stacie tried to block the blows with her right arm as she desperately tried to grab hold of Debbie's arm with her free hand. Stacie screamed out in fear, but her cries went unheard as Debbie overpowered her. Again, Debbie struck Stacie with the candlestick holder—the one with the little monkey that covered his eyes from all evil—and this time Debbie hit her on the top of the head, making Stacie's eyes fill with blotches of small, discolored stars. Stacie broke away from Debbie, and tried desperately to reach the solarium.

"Debbie...please...stop...I'm–" Stacie's voice was low, and her words didn't flow as they did minutes before. Stacie could taste blood in her mouth as she struggled towards the solarium, and when she reached the room, she fell to the floor.

Debbie was right behind her, but Stacie was surrounded by a void of darkness. In her mind, Debbie saw Stacie kick at her from the floor. Debbie moved, but not before throwing the heavy candlestick holder at the back of Stacie's head. Debbie looked down as Stacie and she could see blood saturating her sister's once beautiful blond hair. Debbie saw what she had done, yet found it difficult to recall.

Debbie stood over Stacie's motionless body still holding the candlestick holder. She saw it in her hands; she had not thrown it like she had thought, but had instead repeatedly beat Stacie with it until her head had split open. Debbie couldn't open her hand to release the heavy object—an innocent object that had been used as a weapon.

She held it up in front of her face and looked at the small monkey with his hands over his eyes. Its little bronze face and hands were covered in blood, and the longer Debbie gazed at the monkey, the more Stacie bled onto the hardwood floor.

Debbie couldn't move, and then something happened that broke her dreamy gaze from that monkey's face: blood touched her. Stacie's blood slowly made its way down the monkey's face, and trickled even slower in a thin stream down the handle. It then touched Debbie's thumb, making her release her grip; slowly, the candlestick fell towards the floor, and when it hit the hard surface, she thought of Jason looking at it on that day when she first brought him to the beach house.

See no evil... Debbie thought.

She couldn't help but ask herself why she had reached for that candlestick. Out of all the candlestick holders that sat on that large wooden table, she picked that one.

"Stacie," she said as the monkey sat in Stacie's small pool of blood around her head. "Stacie! *No...no...* no! Stacie, look at me! Stacie! Stacie!"

Debbie had fallen to her knees, and rolled Stacie over to examine her face and eyes. There was nothing that betrayed life within Stacie's body. Her lips and nose were smeared with blood, and strands of Stacie's hair were sticking to her face. The longer Debbie studied the lifeless face of her sister, the more it didn't resemble her sibling at all.

Debbie wept uncontrollably as she tried to wake her up, but she knew Stacie wouldn't come back to her. Suddenly, a horrifying feeling came over her, and she pushed herself away from Stacie's body. Debbie's feet slipped in the blood as she moved herself up against the wall. That fear didn't stop; it followed her and crept back into her mind.

I killed her. I killed her. I killed my sister. Why? Why...?

Debbie knew the answer, but couldn't say it out loud. She feared a lot more than just that thought. She thought of her father and what he would say, and she thought of her mother who once told her that she loved them both. Debbie knew right then and there that she would have to move Stacie outside somewhere, and that was all she could think of. Debbie was having a hard time thinking clearly; she didn't realize that she could just leave Stacie there on the floor, and come up with some kind of account as to what had happened.

Debbie pulled Stacie by her feet and dragged her outside. Stacie felt heavy, like a log that had been afloat in the ocean for several days. Debbie could feel that sick feeling returning to her stomach as she let go of Stacie's feet. They hit the sand with a thud—like a bag of flour hitting the kitchen floor and splitting open—pain could be felt inside her stomach again. She turned away from Stacie, feeling like she was going to be sick, and not understanding why she had not left Stacie where she had fallen. She had panicked after realizing that she had just killed her, and now that feeling came back to her.

What am I going to do with her? Where can...should I move her? Where should I move her? I...maybe...

Debbie's judgment was impaired; it was the lack of pills--her doctor had warned her of this. She looked around, and could see nowhere that she could hide her. There were the boat docks, but they were too far away. Debbie suddenly remembered something—something that only she and Stacie knew from their childhood. It would mean doing a little more than just moving Stacie … but it would be the last time.

19

Visiting hours were extended for Peg; after all, it wasn't everyday that Richard awoke from a coma. She was allowed to stay a half hour longer, and then she would have to say her goodbyes. They held hands the whole time, and she kissed him lovingly as many times as she could within her stay.

Richard gazed up at her, as if she was a star that mesmerized him at night. She was beautiful for a woman of her age, and it seemed like he hadn't laid eyes on her in months.

"Are you going to bring the girls the next time you come?" Richard asked in a weak voice.

"Yes, maybe tomorrow, or the next day," she responded as if she was unsure; she still did not have any idea what was going on up at the beach house.

Just then, a nurse came into the room and asked Richard if he was okay. The nurse said that he would have to get some rest before he started physiotherapy tomorrow morning. The nurse told him that they were going to work on getting his strength up, so that he could be released as soon as possible. Peg gave Richard one last kiss goodbye, and then stood to turn when Richard grabbed her by the hand.

"I love you," he said.

"I love you more," she replied with a loving smile, and turned to leave.

As soon as she was out of the hospital, she tried to call Debbie. But Debbie did not answer. Peg could only hope that Debbie was able to get Stacie out of the house like she had asked her to. She kept trying Debbie's cell, but there was still no answer. All Peg could do was wonder what was going on up at the beach house.

* * *

Debbie looked down at her hands as she walked back into the house; the dead hallway lights kept her from seeing all the blood that her hands had gathered, yet when she stepped into areas that held some light from outside, she saw just how much blood was on her hands, her shirt, and her blue denim jeans. Debbie turned her hands over and over. She looked at the tops of her hands longer than the palms of them; there was more blood on the outside of them, and it was hard to look at it in the dismal light, but she could feel its thickness.

Debbie turned to the stairs and looked all the way up. She was moving slowly; she was still stunned. Debbie felt like she was walking through an underwater dream, and at any moment she would wake up from this nightmare. But this was no dream, however; it was a nightmare.

Debbie climbed the stairs and went into the washroom were she washed her hands over and over again. That white sink became stained with Stacie's blood. Debbie scrubbed her hands harder as she watched herself in the dim mirror. Her face looked drained of all its life, and she had dead eyes. Her pupils were three times their normal size—like dolls' eyes—and she saw blood on the side of her face.

Debbie touched the mirror with a slow and steady hand, as if the glass was going to move like water and show her that the blood was really on the mirror and not on her face. She touched the mirror, but the blood was not on its surface; it was on the surface of her skin. She snapped out of her daze and began frantically splashing water on her face. Debbie scrubbed and scrubbed, and even though she got the blood off her hands and face, it was still in the sink, and on the white hand towel that hung near the mirror. She knew it would never go away; it would always be in her mind. Like the stain in the sink, like the burn on an old photograph—it would always be in her mind.

Debbie cleaned up the best she could and then let the bar of soap fall freely to the countertop; it now held the markings of blood, but these marks looked like veins. It reminded her of blood in the snow. They were light, and a little hard to see.

She walked out of the bathroom and spotted colored paper on the floor; she knew that Stacie had dropped them. Debbie turned to the open door and looked into her mother's room, but didn't enter. Debbie picked up the colored paper as she kept an eye on the open door. She looked at the paper and saw that they were letters; she began to read them the best she could in the dim light.

Richard … we will be together now, forever. I love when you call me your, 'little-Peggy-baby.' You're my sweetheart. You always will be dear to my heart.

Debbie let the letter fall to the floor, and then read the next one. It held the same feel as the first one, it read: **I love when he holds me. I forget about everything that makes me unhappy, and sad.**

Richard. Richard. Richard. I'm finally with the only man I have ever loved, and will ever love.

Debbie didn't let this one fall out of her hands like the last letter. She held it tight and saw something that Stacie had overlooked. There was a date in the top right hand corner. It was dated, May 17, 1989, and again, there was Peg's name.

Debbie fell into a deep thought, and couldn't believe what she was reading. She knew that she would have been around seven that year, and that was also the year that aunt Peg went missing. She quickly went into her mother's room and tried her best to look around. Debbie saw the shattered glass that was once in the shape of a jar, and the hair that it held. She picked it up without knowing exactly what she was handling; the room was dark, and the only light was from outside. The glow of the moonlight and those street lights up on the main road shone into the house as if they were shining into the murky abyss of an ocean, helping her see just a little. Debbie held it up to her face and understood what she was holding.

"Is this hair?" She dropped it and rubbed her hands on her shirt with disgust. She then saw the ribbon with the name Margaret on it.

"Stacie was right. She was trying to tell me something important, and I wouldn't listen." Debbie couldn't believe it. She left the room and sat on the top step sobbing into her hands.

"Stacie! Stacie!" Debbie cried out. She wished now that her mind would become unclear like it had before, because her thoughts were too much to bear, and she could not keep them at bay.

Debbie had forgotten all about the blood in the solarium, and the back door that was wide open. She did, however, remember the paper that Stacie was trying to show her; trying to get her to read. Debbie pulled herself up by the wooden handrails, and she felt like she was going to vomit again. She had never felt this way before, but she couldn't help that now. She forced herself downstairs without incident, and over to where the letters had fallen out of Stacie's hand and littered the floor.

Debbie saw no significance like she had seen in the other letters in these letters. They didn't tell her anything more—like why her father had fallen for their aunt—and in a way they didn't have to, because Stacie had done that for her.

Debbie put the letters down and walked into the solarium. She turned her head away from the small pool of blood. She couldn't bring herself to look at it. She could see Stacie's bloody face in her mind and she didn't want it to appear in the pool of blood and call out to her, like she knew it would. Debbie knew that that would be more horrifying than what was already lurking inside her head.

The cool night air bit at Debbie's bare arms as she walked out the back door towards the beach. She could almost hear Stacie yelling out to her; telling her about the flowers near the end of the beach. Debbie was trying hard to put it all together, but it was difficult; it was her own actions that had led to this confusion within her mind. She pushed on towards the end of the beach, knowing now that her mother could be out here—her real mother—but she also knew that there was nothing she could do at this late hour. Debbie could barely see her hand in front of her own face as she move further away from the house. She turned and headed back.

Debbie had almost reached the back door when she heard the sound of a car pulling into the driveway, and the light crunching sound of gravel beneath it. Debbie didn't enter the beach house. Instead, she made her way around to the side of it to see who it was, but she already knew. Debbie kept close to the side of the house as she watched the woman who had pretended to be her mother for most of her life step out of her car and head into the house; Debbie then followed.

Peg looked around as she stood in the entrance. She couldn't believe her eyes. She didn't see her letters at first—it was too dark for that—she, however, noticed the kitchen, and then the living room. Everything was out of place. Peg saw one of the colored letters on the floor. She was able to get a good look at it, and it looked to her that there was blood on it. She looked up from the letter and slowly made her way towards the solarium where she could see another letter on the floor just before the doorway.

"What the hell happened here?" Peg said as she stepped into the room. She couldn't see the blood on the floor at first, because all she saw was the color red before her eyes; she was livid. Even the orange paper in her hand looked almost crimson.

"Debbie! Stacie!" She called out as she crumpled the letter in her trembling hands.

In the other room all the candlestick holders were in complete disarray. Peg could see some of them on the floor, but most of them were knocked over on the tabletop; only a few still stood. She couldn't fathom what she was seeing, and then she saw the pool of blood. That's when what had transpired here came to her.

"Debbie! Stacie!" Peg called out again as she turned around. "Debbie?" Peg's voice fell as she stared at her daughter standing right behind her. "What happened here? Are you okay? Where is Stacie?"

"Is it true?" Debbie began to say as she held a couple of letters in her hand, showing them to Peg.

"Debbie, you don't know the facts."

"You're my aunt Peg, not my mother. You made us believe that you were our mother all this time, all these years. How could you? What happened to my mother?" Debbie demanded, slamming the letters down on a small marble table so hard that she made the little lamp on it move from side to side with a soft, rhythmic wobble.

"There's a lot you don't know, and I'm sorry, but I did it to protect the family," Peg told her as she moved to her left. "Those letters are mine…only I can explain them."

"What happened to my mother?"

"Nothing. Nothing happened to her," Peg replied as she turned back to the blood. "Debbie…where is Stacie? You still haven't answered me. I would like to talk to her as well."

Debbie's face dropped as her emotions took hold of her. That agony filled her heart again, and all she could do was cover her face with her hands again,

"Oh my, God. You… you killed her?"

"I…" Debbie began to speak through her sobs, "I didn't mean for it to go so far, but I couldn't stop myself," Debbie sobbed even heavier as she broke down.

"Debbie, it's okay," Peg said as she walked over to her. Debbie's hands were still hiding her face in shame, and did not see Peg pick up the letters as she approached her.

"It's not okay," Debbie said, removing her hands and looking up at Peg.

"You're wrong. Don't you see? With Stacie gone, and your father awake, you will get everything if I ever pass away, and now we can be one family, just the three of us."

"So, this is all about the will. Dad's will?" Debbie asked, taking a step back from her aunt. "You don't care what has happened here. What could happen to me?"

"In a way, yes. I care and love you, and nothing is going to happen to you. No one ever has to know what has taken place here tonight. You still don't see it, do you, Debbie? You're an only child. Stacie was your stepsister. Your father wasn't married to me when you were born."

Debbie looked at her with bewilderment in her eyes. She could hear what she was trying to say, but found it hard to comprehend it.

"You get it all. Your father is alive, thank God. He can talk to you about this when he is up and about. You were his first born, but your aunt Margaret did not know that your father and I held love for one another. She—"

"Stop! I don't want to hear this. It's all lies. It doesn't even make any sense. I still wouldn't get anything, because father is alive and...you are alive," Debbie said, as she thought about it deep inside. "You took my mother's identity, so that you could be on the will, but Stacie would have to die before you or I got anything, but only if father dies as well," Debbie said, taking another step back.

"I did it because I love your father, and he loves me. I did it for you, because you're my little girl. I never wanted you to find out this way. I never knew how to tell you."

"It's not hard to tell a lie, aunt Peg," Debbie said.

"I told you, I'm not your aunt."

"Yes you are, and Stacie was right about you. I know now that you killed our mother, maybe the police should know as well."

"You and I have both made mistake in life, Debbie, but like I said, I did it because I love your father and he loves me," she said, as Debbie looked back at her. Debbie would never be able to rectify what she had done; she knew that what she had done hadn't hit her fully at that moment, but in time, it would unfold with pain.

"But I'm able to prove what you call a mistake, and show you who you really are," Debbie said, heading outside to her car.

Peg followed her.

"Where are you going, and where the hell is your sister!" Peg yelled out. Her words cut into Debbie like a dull knife; the pain was almost enough to make her stop and fall to her knees again.

Debbie reached into her pocket and pulled out her car keys as she looked behind her. Peg was advancing on her, walking as fast as she could.

"Debbie, please stop and talk to me. We can talk about this."

"I have nothing to say to you. You lied to us all these years," Debbie said as she opened the car door.

"Where are you going to go? Peg asked. She was now close enough to Debbie that she could slow down. "Debbie…wait," she said as she took hold of her arm.

"Don't touch me!" Debbie yelled out, quickly removing Peg's hand. "You can talk all you want when the police come for you," Debbie remarked as she went to slip into the car seat.

"You're not going to call anyone!" Peg said in a raised voice. She grabbed Debbie's arm again—this time harder than before—and made her drop her keys into the dark grass.

Peg kicked at them, not knowing exactly where they were, as Debbie tried to push her away.

"Debbie. Sit in your car and listen to what I have to say," Peg asked of her, but Debbie wouldn't hear of it.

Peg kicked the grass again. It was as dark as a moonless lake. Her foot hit something that made a clanging sound—like chains—and went under the car.

"Debbie reached for her handbag, and Peg knew that her cell phone was in it.

"You're not going to call anyone," Peg reiterated, but she was too far from Debbie to reach her handbag.

Debbie began to run from the car and away from Peg. Debbie pulled the phone from her bag, and looked at the screen. Two missed calls, it read. She bypassed the screen and tried to call out, but couldn't.

Debbie looked behind her and could see that Peg was close, then just as quickly as she looked behind her, she turned back and looked at her phone again.

"Come on!" She said in frustration. Her signal was low. "Damn it."

"Debbie, please…hear me out. We wouldn't be going through this if it weren't for your sister," she began to say, and Debbie slowed down a little.

Debbie looked around. She was unsure of where she should go to get away from Peg, and then she saw the streetlights up on the road. She began to run towards the stone stairway as Peg did her best to keep up.

"You will regret this, Debbie. If you call the police, you will regret this. They will question all of us, just like the last time when Stacie was hit by that car and didn't die. You will burn for what you have done," she yelled out.

Debbie reached the stairs, turned towards Peg, and thought for a moment. She remembered that time when Stacie was almost run down by a man in a black car. Stacie always thought that someone had set it up, but could never prove it.

"You tried to kill her that time…didn't you?" Debbie asked with a look of shock on her face.

Peg was hesitant with her answer, but it slowly came out. "…Yes."

"Why? I…" Debbie couldn't say anything more. She stood frozen at the front of the dark stairs.

"Because she is not my daughter, and it had to be done. After that first failed attempt, I just couldn't get anyone to try that again. You have done what I couldn't finish. You have succeeded where I have failed; I know that it's true, because all that blood is not yours. That is easy to see."

Debbie began to make her way up the stairs; she didn't want to hear anymore. Peg didn't let her get very far; she followed close behind her.

"Give me the phone, Debbie," Peg said, trying to grab hold of one of Debbie's ankles.

Those steps were steep and not very wide. They only had one landing halfway up. Debbie was almost at that landing when she felt a hand grab hold of her foot, and then the other hand could be felt grabbing hold of her ankle.

"Let me go!" Debbie shouted, kicking at Peg

There was no railing to hold onto, and if Peg were to fall, Debbie would surely fall as well and suffer an injury. She tried to pull her foot free of Peg's grip, but she couldn't, and as she placed her left hand on the next step, a large part of it gave way. Debbie slipped and hit her head on the step below her hand as the piece of the stone step rolled past Peg, almost striking her.

"Debbie, give me the phone. We don't have to do this."

All Debbie could hear was ringing in her head as she held onto the step. Her head filled with pain, and her thoughts became sluggish.

Peg could see that Debbie was hurt, and that she had dropped the phone from her right hand. It had fallen just below Debbie's elbow about three steps down; Peg pulled on Debbie's foot to help herself up to the next step.

"You're not going to call anyone. I'm your mother," Peg said, out of breath.

Debbie's head throbbed with an uneven pulsation of pain, and as she saw Peg coming up the steps, she kicked at her with her free foot. Peg moved to avoid being kicked in the head, but Debbie underestimated how serious Peg was, and before Debbie could kick at her again, Peg twisted Debbie's foot as hard as she could, breaking the talus bone and the tibia, and her ankle.

Debbie screamed in sheer pain and her voice carried through the night air. Pain shot up her leg and almost made her lose her grip again.

"Get off me!" Debbie yelled, kicking Peg right in the face with the heel of her other foot. Peg lost her hold on Debbie's broken ankle and fell backwards down the jagged stone stairway.

Debbie took a moment and tried to reach down to touch her ankle to get a feel on how badly it was broken, but couldn't. She looked down the stairs at Peg, who had fallen, but it was hard to see her. Perhaps if the streetlights were moved directly over the stairs with a little more light to see into that darkness below, then she would be able to tell if she was alive.

Debbie shifted slowly as the pain moved up and down her leg like electricity through a cable line. She had to keep going; she could hear the cars on the street just above the next set of steps. However, she wouldn't be able to get through the gate that stood before the sidewalk. Debbie could feel her head pulsating again like a pink balloon, ready to burst at any moment.

Another car could be heard going by. There wouldn't be a lot, and she knew it. The houses here were far apart from each other. She heard someone talking, but she didn't know if it was in her head or on the other side of the gate.

"I love you. I love you," she could hear the voice say.

"Help," Debbie called out to what sounded like a couple walking by. She heard it again, and it was then that she pinpointed where the voice was coming from. She turned her head and saw Peg coming up the stairs with that piece of the stone step in her hands.

Debbie rolled over to better defend herself, but found it difficult to roll herself over completely without feeling extreme pain.

"I love you, but you leave me no choice," Peg said as she threw the stone at Debbie.

It grazed the side of her head, and Debbie saw fuzzy shapes in front of her eyes. Peg grabbed Debbie's hair and pulled her forward and then slammed the back of her head into the step. Debbie slowly slipped into darkness, and her eyes could only see more blurred images.

Peg picked up the stone and stood over Debbie.

"No," Debbie uttered in a weak voice, She could see a shadow standing over her. Debbie knew that it was Peg standing over her, and feared for her life; she could only hope that her death would be quick and painless.

Debbie opened her eyes the best she could, and saw Peg's shadow move from right to left, and then she heard a scream that sounded like her aunt. That scream filled Debbie's head.

"No...please," Debbie pleaded in a voice so quiet that even she couldn't hear herself. Debbie saw nothing but colors and images of odd shapes in her head as she closed her eyes, and a feeling of floating away came over her.

So, this is death. This is how it feels, she thought as she floated away beyond darkness.

20

Muffled sounds could be heard from two tall shadowy figures moving from side to side. They were trying to form words between them in the darkness. One of the shadows moved towards the foreground and the other one stayed behind. The shadow stayed at bay, and it morphed into the darker, colorless shapes around it.

"Morning," the shadow in the foreground said, shoving away its muffled voice.

Debbie's eyes were only open a little, but soon closed after a tall thin nurse with long dark hair opened the shades to let the morning sun fill the room. After a minute, Debbie slowly opened her eyes again, taking in the rays of light. It helped her see the other nurse standing over by the doorway. She looked at Debbie and smiled, and then looked back down at her clipboard.

"How...long..." Debbie tried to talk, but found that her jaw was sore.

"No, no. You just rest," the nurse told her. " You have been here for two days—this one will make it your third," she told Debbie with a chuckle. "You're going to be fine. You're a lucky girl. You'll have to stay under our care for about two weeks, maybe less. We're going to have to keep an eye on your head wounds," she told Debbie.

"How did. I get here?" Debbie asked.

"Sorry, I don't work the night shift, and I'm a fill-in for today on this floor," the nurse replied. She said goodbye and told Debbie that she would be back in an hour with her pills.

"My pills?" Debbie asked as the nurse walked out of the room.

The other nurse with the clipboard walked over to Debbie's bedside, and started flipping through papers.

"Citalopram," she began to say, "for depression, and Tramadol, for pain. Your ankle was badly broken."

"How do you know about my depression?" Debbie asked, trying to get up, but her pain wouldn't let her.

"Your friend told the night shift nurse when he brought you in."

"What friend?" Debbie asked in pain.

"Sorry I can't remember his name right know," she said as she looked at Debbie's face. It was heartbreaking to watch. "I'm sorry. I'll ask at the front desk, maybe they have the name of the person that brought you in."

"Okay," Debbie said as she turned her head towards the window.

I remember two missed calls, Debbie thought as the nurse left the room.

"Jason," Debbie said suddenly. The nurse turned and walked back over to Debbie and looked down at her.

"Yes…I think that was the gentleman's name. Yes, that was his name, now that I think of it," she said as she looked at Debbie and saw her face light up a little after hearing it confirmed by the nurse.

"He is a good friend," the nurse asked as she adjusted Debbie's pillow.

"He was," Debbie said, and her face fell dark.

"I think, if it wasn't for him, I wouldn't be having this conversation with you right now," the nurse said.

Debbie knew that it was true, and that the nurse was right.

"He told us you fell down a dirt hill when you were out on your midnight run," the nurse told her.

"…Yes. I was upset and went for a run. He called and I answered the phone while I was still running, and that's all I can remember."

"Well you're lucky he called you when he did, and you shouldn't go out running at night with all those cars racing around, and all the nuts running around as well."

"You're right," Debbie said as the nurse left the room.

* * *

Lewis Thompson finished his tea and called his prize-winning Great Danes for their morning walk.

He was leaving earlier then usual, because he couldn't sleep.

"Come on, girls," he called out as he jiggled their silver chain leashes.

Queenie and Missy came running. He got them ready and then opened the front door. It was so nice out; the fresh morning air held the hint of fall, but it was still nice enough to walk without a sweater. He just needed a light jacket and tee-shirt.

They went to the park and then up to the beach, but not on the beach. All the houses on this side were large and had their own private beaches. Lewis never liked that. He always saw it as another way for the rich to turn their backs on the part of the world that didn't stand as tall as the other people of his level. But he loved looking at the ocean when he walked the dogs near the hill overlooking the clear water, which, in its own way, emulated light green glass.

"Come on, girls," he said as he walked up Beach Avenue, and then down the one-way street.

Lewis looked up at the stone wall that abruptly switched to a wall of thick iron fence with spear points all along the top. There were bushes and trees on the other side, and some of them had grown through the spacing of the fence.

Queenie began to pull Lewis forward as they neared a part of the fence that had no bush behind it, and as they got closer, Missy began to bark and paw at the iron fence. Queenie started to bark as well, and when Lewis looked at the fence, he saw that it was actually a gate, and it was locked.

"Calm down, girls. What is it?" Lewis looked at the beach and all its beauty, and then over at the beach house that seemed so far away. It was a steep hill, and he wondered why anyone would put a gate all the way up here.

"Come, girls. Let's go," he said walking past them as they barked and scratched at the black iron bars.

Lewis couldn't understand what had gotten into them. He went back over to the gate and tried to pull them by their collars, but they wouldn't have it. There was something on the other side of that gate that they could see.

"You girls see another dog?" Lewis asked them as he examined the hill again. He saw the stone stairs, and knew that that was the reason for the gate.

He didn't notice the stone stairs the first time he looked though the gate. Lewis's eyes followed the path of the steps all the way to the bottom where a small tree stood, and as he scanned the grass, he saw something protruding out from underneath it. It was hard to make out at first, but then he saw that it was a human leg.

"Dear, God," Lewis didn't call out to the person; the dogs had done that for him already.

"Good, girls," Lewis said. "We have to go back to the hose. Come on," he told them as he pulled them away from the gate.

They moved away from the gate, and Lewis rushed back to the house, where he then called the police.

* * *

Debbie made a pot of coffee and sat in the kitchen of the mansion as she looked out the window. She had been home—her new home for now—for only a day, and all she could think of was her itchy foot. She knew that cast would come off in time, but this was her first time ever having a broken bone, and this was all new to her.

Her friend Kim had picked her up from the hospital. Debbie couldn't bring herself to ask Jason, and even though he had rescued her from certain death, she found it hard to pick up the phone and call him to thank him for what he had done, let alone ask him for anything; Stacie was, in a way, deep in her thoughts, holding her back.

Jason had done more then just save her from her mother, and take her to the hospital. He had moved her car with all her bags in it from the beach house to the mansion. She wasn't sure at first why he had done it, or how he had done it, but what she knew was that he had done it for her. It then came to her; she knew that if anything were to come from that night, that it would all point to her, and that it would be her own car that would point the way. As she took her pills, she held the thought of him close to her heart in spite of what he had done. She put the bottle down on the table beside a Center for Depression card that was given to her by one of the nurses as she was being discharged. She hoped that they would be able to help with her sickness, as well as the nausea from her medication, if that was what it was from.

She finished her coffee and went out onto the back deck. She hated those crutches, but she would have to live with them for the next six weeks.

Debbie sat down and enjoyed the peaceful morning as she went through her phone, and it was then that she thought about the two missed calls. She checked the numbers; they were both from Jason. She then noticed that she had one unread text. She wanted to read it, but at the same time she didn't. She touched the icon on the screen and opened the text. It read: *Left keys in bag.*

It was from Jason. She closed her eyes and thought of only the good times that they once shared, and wondered if things could ever be that way again. She got up and limped down the small set of steps to the grass.

Debbie found it a little easier to walk on the grass than on solid ground. She walked around to the side of the house. She sat down on the stone bench and let the warm air take her away, yet her rest didn't last long. Debbie had just closed her eyes for a moment when she heard a car pull up outside the gates.

Debbie opened her eyes and saw two men wearing suits get out of a cream-colored car. One of the men stood taller than the other, and had on a dark, navy-blue suit with a tie that did not match it whatsoever; the other gentleman was wearing a light gray suit. There was no tie; instead, he had the first three buttons of his shirt open and his jacket open all the way. He looked much younger then the taller man. He seemed to be overwhelmed by the size of the house and the grounds, and the gate that he stood in front of.

"Hello," the tall, dark-haired man said as he looked at Debbie through the gate.

"Can I help you?" Debbie replied, getting up slowly from the bench with a cringe on her face; her ankle was sore and with a little pain, it reminded her that it was still broken.

"We would like to speak with a Richard Whiting," the taller man said as Debbie hobbled over to the gate. He then introduced himself. "I'm detective Dickson, and this is my partner detective Dean."

"My father isn't home," Debbie told the two detectives as she tried to keep her balance.

"When do you expect him home?" Dean stepped forward and asked.

"A week, or so. It could be longer. However long it takes the hospital to release him. He just came out of a coma, about a week ago," she told them, yet she was looking at detective Dean when she said it. "You haven't showed me a badge yet, nor have you told me what this is all about," Debbie responded with eyes that showed them that it hurt her to stand.

"Maybe you can answer a couple of questions for us," detective Dickson asked as he showed her his badge.

Debbie opened the gate and let them in. They walked over to the bench and sat down.

"We just have a couple of things to ask you, and then we will be on our way, so that you get back to your day," Dickson said. "We wanted to talk with your father about a Peggy Bell, and a Margaret Whiting."

"Maiden name, Bell, Margaret Bell," Dean suddenly said, looking in his small notebook.

"Peg is my aunt. Margaret's my mother," Debbie said.

"And when was the last time you spoke with her?" Dickson asked looking around.

"About a week ago. I had a falling out with my boyfriend, and asked her if I could stay here for a while. It must have been my lucky day, because she said yes. She doesn't like it when there are people around."

"This falling out, is that how you broke your leg?" Dean asked.

"God, no. I was running and stepped off the side of the road and fell down a small embankment," Debbie told him. "Is my father in some kind of trouble?" Debbie then quickly asked, not wanting to talk about her leg any longer.

Both Dickson and Dean looked at each other and then back at Debbie.

"We have reason to believe that Peggy Bell has been living her life as her sister, Margaret Whiting, and that your father knows something about it," Dickson told her. "He would have to know," he then added.

"That can't be. My aunt went missing years ago," Debbie said showing them that she didn't want to believe was she was hearing.

"I don't think you fully understand what we are trying to say," Dean replied.

She did. She knew all too well, but she was *not* going to let them know that.

"Miss Whiting, we believe that your aunt Peg murdered your birth mother years ago. We're sorry. We're also sorry to inform you that she herself has been murdered at your family's beach house," Dickson told her.

Debbie's head dropped into her hands as she thought of Stacie and cried. She shook her head from side to side, thinking only of Stacie.

"We are deeply sorry, but this is why we must talk with your father, because he must have known about your aunt," Dean reiterated what his partner had already told her.

Debbie calmed herself as she looked at them. She told them what hospital he was in.

"There is just one other thing," Dickson began to say, "your sister is Stacie Amy Whiting?"

"Yes," Debbie responded.

"We would *really* like to have a word with her. If you hear from her can you let her know that we wish to have a talk with her, and that we may be stopping by her residence?"

"Yes, if I see her. She hasn't done anything wrong, has she?" Debbie asked knowing that they must feel that Stacie had something to do with Peg's death, because of her car being at the beach house.

They both stood up, and Dickson said, "Thank you for your time, and again, we are truly sorry."

They both said goodbye and saw themselves out without answering Debbie's question.

21

Two months had passed without a single drink. Debbie was now going to the Center for Depression two times a week, and trying to get her life back on track. She knew it would be hard, but she also knew that she could get though it with a little help.

Detectives Dickson and Dean had been back to talk with Richard after he returned home. They questioned him about Peg. Richard told them that Margaret had left him after she found out about his affair with her sister, and that was around the time Peg moved in with him. Richard said that he knew absolutely nothing about Peg living a double life as her sister.

Richard couldn't tell them that he knew Margaret was missing, because he had never reported it to the police. Richard loved Peg, yet was so grief-stricken when Margaret left him (went missing), and that was when he turned to Peg. Richard told Debbie that Peg never wanted him to file a missing person's report on Margaret, but for them to file one for Peg. He loved her so much and did what she asked. With Debbie only six years old at the time, he did what he felt was right to keep she and her sister together … and to keep Peg by his side. Debbie and Stacie grew up knowing her only as Mom. Debbie looked at her father with wide eyes as he told her about the past.

"So she was telling me the truth," Debbie said, looking at him. "She told me that she was my mother, but … I just didn't believe her."

"It should never have been that way, but that's how it happened. I loved her and you girls, and she loved us. You came to live with me because your mother couldn't watch you the way you should've been watched, and that environment was not right for a small child, so she asked me and Margaret if we would take care of you for a while so that she could get her problems under control," he explained to her.

"Her problems?"

"Yes. She suffered from depression, just like you, but when she got over it she wanted you and I to be together. I told her that I couldn't, because of Stacie, and then two weeks later Margaret woke up before I did, and left the house for some reason. I never saw or heard from her again. That same day, Peg called off and on asking for her, and when days turned into a week, I knew something must have happened to her. Peg was there to comfort me," Richard told Debbie with his head down.

Debbie didn't say anything. She didn't feel anything. She had killed her sister out of love and uncontrollable anger just like her mother had done to her own sister.

"Do you know what happened?" Debbie asked, knowing the answer, but wanting to hear it from him.

"No. But I always had a feeling that Peg had something to do with Margaret's disappearance. Peg always said that no one cared about her, and that if she went missing that all the police would find was an old house. I went along with it because I didn't want to lose you girls. I would have gone to jail just like her if they found out that she was living the life of her missing sister."

"I understand," Debbie said, putting her arm around him. "I always thought you never cared."

"I care. I care about you both, and now Stacie is gone, and the police suspect her of murder," he said as tears streamed down the side of his cheeks. "I should have told you two so many years ago, but I just… didn't know how to."

"It's going to be okay," Debbie said as she held him with no emotion.

"Debbie, do you know where she is? I would like to talk to her, and tell her I'm not mad, and that she can come back home."

"No...I don't know where she has gone. She hasn't called me. She may never call me, after what she has done."

Richard didn't say anything as he held his cup of coffee in both hands, and gazed at the swirling pale brown rings within the black coffee mug.

"I have to go and pick up a couple of things at the store. Do you need anything?" Debbie asked. Debbie could tell that this was not going to be an easy time for her father. He looked so empty without Stacie near him, but showed some life when he looked up at her.

"No, thank you. I'm okay. I would like to cook tonight, though," he told her. "You have cooked for me the last five nights, so I would like to cook for you. Maybe your friend can come over," Richard suggested.

"My friend? You mean Jason?"

"Yes. Is that the person you had coffee with the other day?"

"Yes," she said, looking at the time on her phone, and checking to see if there were any missed calls. "Well, I better get going," she said.

Debbie drove out to the beach house after getting what she needed at the store. She parked on the side of the road just before it turned into the gravel driveway. She was able to see the sun glittering on the ocean as it slowly swayed back and forth, showing its true sparkling allure. Debbie thought of Stacie, and only Stacie.

Debbie couldn't see any police tape as her eyes turned towards the beach house. She looked at it in a way that she had never looked at it before, and she knew then that it would never look the same way ever again. All she saw were the panels on the side of the house, and the one just below the kitchen window slightly obscured by the rose bushes.

"Come on, Debbie."

She could hear Stacie's voice in her head as clear as day, so clear that it was as if Stacie was whispering into Debbie ear from the backseat of the car.

"Come on, hurry, before Daddy finds us."

Debbie could see two young girls—transparent like smoke dissipating into the air—playing by the side of the house near the rose bushes.

"Hurry. Hurry. Dad is coming."

Debbie could hear her own voice in her own head; it was so soft and vivid as if she was speaking those words for the first time. She could almost see her father coming around to the side of the house and standing right near the rose bushes, but the vision of him faded away.

"Where did my girls go?"

Debbie remembered how he would say that, and how he was so oblivious to where they had gone. She also remembered the way they would giggle with their hands over their mouths to muffle their laughter as they sat watching him through a small hole from their secret hiding place. Debbie reminisced about those days and how he never once found them. Just then, as she was deep in thought, her phone vibrated in her bag; it was a text from Jason.

Hope you are okay. Hope we can talk again soon. Thank you for coffee the other day. Hope to see you soon. Do not want to lose your friendship. P.S. Cleaned up the best I could.

Debbie looked back at the house and knew right away what Jason was trying to tell her. Debbie put the phone down and could no longer see the image of her and Stacie. She looked out at the ocean, and then turned towards the side of house and the rose bushes one last time. Debbie wiped a tear from her eye, and thought about how she and Stacie are still—in a way—hiding from their father behind that loose panel at the side of the house behind the rosebushes. Debbie felt a dull ache at how she and Stacie had gone down the same road as their mother and aunt. Debbie realized that she has followed in her mother's footsteps, and that she would have to live with the scent of rosebushes, and the smell of the earth from under the beach house until she came to the end of that road herself.

"Goodbye," Debbie said in a soft voice, without saying her sister's name, and then put the car in drive, and headed towards home.

CPSIA information can be obtained at www.ICGtesting.com
Printed in the USA
LVOW06s0321170914

404368LV00005B/24/P